NOVELS BY ERIC PETE

Lady Sings the Cruels

Don't Get It Twisted

Gets No Love

ERIC PETE

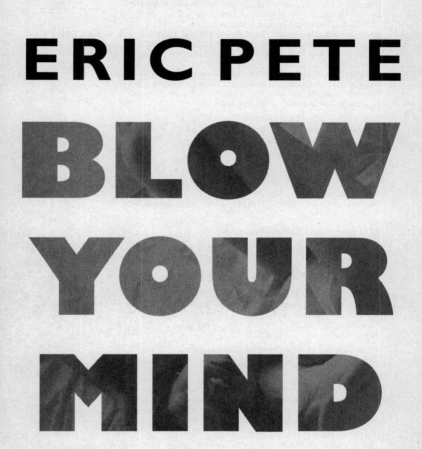

BLOW YOUR MIND

NEW AMERICAN LIBRARY

New American Library
Published by New American Library, a division of
Penguin Group (USA) Inc., 375 Hudson Street,
New York, New York 10014, USA
Penguin Group (Canada), 90 Eglinton Avenue East, Suite 700, Toronto,
Ontario M4P 2Y3, Canada (a division of Pearson Penguin Canada Inc.)
Penguin Books Ltd., 80 Strand, London WC2R 0RL, England
Penguin Ireland, 25 St. Stephen's Green, Dublin 2,
Ireland (a division of Penguin Books Ltd.)
Penguin Group (Australia), 250 Camberwell Road, Camberwell, Victoria 3124,
Australia (a division of Pearson Australia Group Pty. Ltd.)
Penguin Books India Pvt. Ltd., 11 Community Centre, Panchsheel Park,
New Delhi - 110 017, India
Penguin Group (NZ), 67 Apollo Drive, Rosedale, North Shore 0745,
Auckland, New Zealand (a division of Pearson New Zealand Ltd.)
Penguin Books (South Africa) (Pty.) Ltd., 24 Sturdee Avenue,
Rosebank, Johannesburg 2196, South Africa

Penguin Books Ltd., Registered Offices:
80 Strand, London WC2R 0RL, England

First published by New American Library,
a division of Penguin Group (USA) Inc.

First Printing, October 2007
10 9 8 7 6 5 4 3 2 1

REGISTERED TRADEMARK—MARCA REGISTRADA

LIBRARY OF CONGRESS CATALOGING-IN-PUBLICATION DATA:

Pete, Eric.
  Blow your mind/Eric Pete.
     p. cm.
  ISBN 978-0-451-22215-2
1. African Americans—Fiction.   2. Man-woman relationships—Fiction.
3. Revenge—Fiction.   I. Title.
PS3616.E83B55   2007
813'.6—dc22   2006102824

Set in Palatino   •   Designed by Elke Sigal

Printed in the United States of America

PUBLISHER'S NOTE
This is a work of fiction. Names, characters, places, and incidents either are the
product of the author's imagination or are used fictitiously, and any resemblance
to actual persons, living or dead, business establishments, events, or locales is
entirely coincidental.
    The publisher does not have any control over and does not assume any responsibility for author or third-party Web sites or their content.

To my Marsha.
To you, who've had more faith in me
than I myself during these times,
I dedicate this book.

Thank you.

ACKNOWLEDGMENTS

How interesting to be at this point. To have begun on a dream, a leap of faith, and a credit card. (Okay. A couple of credit cards.) For it is because of you and the Man upstairs that I have made it to this point, several novels later. No idle boast, but this is a special one you hold in your hands, and I hope the chaos you're about to jump into the middle of leaves you breathless, salivating, and craving more. *Kind of like good sex, huh?* Or crack. But crack is whack. *Stick with the sex.*

To my family and friends, I love you guys. I see you out there. From simply an encouraging word to actively getting the word out, I appreciate all that you've done and continue to do.

Shontea, Jacqueline (Glad you're "on the path," lady), and Jamie. Thanks for being there from the beginning and for taking the time to read and critique this latest monster.

To Kara Cesare, I still remember our first conversation. Each subsequent one has been just as memorable. Continued success to you and everyone at NAL, including Lindsay Nouis, Lisa Mondello, and the whole gang behind the scenes, for taking this walk with me. To Elaine Koster, thanks for bringing it all together during this period.

To all the authors who've paved the way, thanks for inspiring us. Mega-kudos go out to my peers and comrades in the trenches, those who understand the sacrifices made in the name of sharing these stories: Kimberla Lawson Roby, Nancy Gilliam, Mary Morrison, Dwayne S. Joseph, Victor McGlothin, Lolita Files, Karen E. Quinones Miller, Zane, Harold L. Turley II, Jihad, Earl Sewell, ReShonda Tate Billingsley, Pat Tucker, V. Anthony Rivers, Victoria Christopher Murray, Jessica Tilles, Dionne Character, Vincent Alexandria, Brenda L. Thomas, Kendra Norman Bellamy, Janet West Sellars, Naleighna Kai, Vanessa Johnson, Yolanda M. Johnson, Claudia Brown-Mosley, William Fredrick Cooper, Jamise Dames, John A. Wooden, Sofia Quintero, Electa Rome Parks, and Cydney Rax.

I have to recognize those in the media—be it print, television, radio, or Internet—who have always been so receptive. An ultraspecial shout-out goes to: Adai Lamar and the KJLH Home Team, Kevin Nash, Erik Tee, Gina Cook, Magic Mike and Big Boy Chill from 107JAMZ, Michael Addison, Gail Norris, Mista Madd, Monica Pierre,

Hal Clark, Angela Jenkins, Jackie Simien, Cheryl Smith, Kelder Summers, Ken Gibbs Jr., Silver Fox, Shelia Goss, Charlotte Morgan, Glenn Townes, LeighAnne Boyd, Shunda Leigh, Angie Pickett-Henderson, Jason McDonald, Shanel Odum, and Kandi Eastman.

To all clubs, readers, and reviewers of books, your love of our written words and worlds means the world. And the world says back, *"Merci, gracias, grazie, xie xie."*

To the booksellers who do this out of love when fortune could be easily sought elsewhere, thank you for sticking with us. May your shelves continue to be lined with the ink from our pens.

Susan Farris, thank you for answering my strange questions about broken fingers 'n' stuff. Trust, there's a method to the madness.

I promised myself that these acknowledgments wouldn't be as long as the last one, so if I missed anyone near and dear, it wasn't intentional. Next time, ginkgo martinis on me.

Friends, see you out there in the world and on MySpace (www.myspace.com/authorericpete), for we have big things ahead.

Look! Up in the sky!

It's a bird!

It's a plane!

Naw . . . just a brother with a sick imagination. Come on up. The weather's fine.

So as the screen fades to black, the girl with the sexy accent whispers, *"This has been another Eric Pete production."*

Roll credits.

Can't stop. Won't stop. Believe that.

1

HENRY

A gun.

A tool like anything else.

Kind of like the stapler or other supplies strewn about in the box in my trunk. A nameplate, an engraved pen—minuscule things I used to value so much, but which were rendered worthless with two words—*You're fired.*

Yes, a gun was a tool. And I was going to answer with a word of my own. Actually, more like a sound.

The sixth floor was illuminated. Besides a red Range Rover, mine was the only car in the employee parking lot. He still was in his office. Figuring how best to ruin other lives, no doubt. I looked at my TAG Heuer golf watch again. No more golf privileges for me. I would probably pawn it if I lived.

If I *chose* to live. Choice is the important component. Something I lost when my gambling seized control of me. Something I didn't have earlier today when that smug bastard sauntered over to my desk with an entourage of building security. The humiliation was enough to send me careening over the edge. Paraded past my peers like a circus monkey.

Oh, that's Henry. He's so bright. If only I had his brains.

They thought I wasn't listening. I heard it all.

He was so dumb. What was he thinking, taking that money?

I was going to kill myself. One bullet.

Right here.

In the parking lot of the job that had defined who I was in this town. No gossip or smirks to endure. Maybe it would create more questions for him to answer. Maybe they'd comb through his finances. He probably had enough skeletons to fill a whole wing, let alone a closet. The bottle of Scotch I held in my lap was to numb me in preparation. By the fifth gulp, I felt less like using the bullet on myself. The burn was doing me good.

It was cold outside. The falling rain was turning to sleet as the night went on. I let another gulp of liquid courage pass my lips, then patted the cold metal on the seat. Funny how my hands marred its shine; perfection ruined by my slight touch. The summary of my life—of addictions spiraling out of control, ruining what could've been. Shit. I *was* the shit. I glowered at my splinted digit. For now, they'd spared my trigger finger.

Small favors.

"Soon," I cooed as if the weapon of death were an eager child instead. Soon my baby would be free to run and play.

But only after I'd made my former employer get off that money.

Yeah, I was a genius at the most unexpected times.

A large Cadillac had sat parked in the semicircle drive since I'd returned from the liquor store. While turning the bottle up, I missed somebody's exit from the building. The car lights surprised me as it roared to life before hastily departing, its tires screaming in protest. It almost clipped my car as it sped past.

Must be getting a ride home tonight, I thought as I hurriedly cranked my own car and put it into drive. The lights on the sixth floor were dimmed. I decided to follow, figuring it was in my best interests.

Weeknight traffic was light, making it easy to trail the car on the winding roads that bordered the river. It was heading toward the old, run-down side of town. Sleet gathered on the fringes of my windshield and, in my intoxicated state, made me check my speed. I could go faster, but the Cadillac would have to slow down.

It didn't.

It kept accelerating.

Right into the harsh curve and through the safety railing.

I saw the sparks flying before I realized what had actually happened. The sound came next, a muffled rumble, followed by a cloud of smoke below. I pulled over several yards back and checked my rearview mirror. Nobody was coming.

I turned off my headlights and exited.

He wasn't getting off that easy. Not after my waiting out in the cold all night. I flung my car door open, gun in hand. The safety was off.

2

MY NAME IS . . .

And I was reborn.

Created anew in an explosion of twisted metal, smoke, and chaos. Emerging from a womb forged in Detroit.

Shards of glass pelted my face, followed by the chill of the rainy night air. The hand that had burst through my window reached for me. In a moment like that, I tried to look in the rearview mirror in some attempt at vanity, but it was gone. Swallowed up in the car's chasm of a floor as the whole vehicle slid toward the rushing waters below.

"What are you doing?"

"I was . . ." What was I doing? As confused as I was, I'd never felt such clarity in my life. Had I really lived before this?

Giving up on reason, he ended the one-sided conversation and snatched me. I felt a tug on my thigh as he fished for a seat belt. I guess I hadn't put it on. Assured, he yanked me through the opening he'd created.

As soon as I was clear, I was cast aside. Tumbling onto the soaked weeds and brush, I watched as he ran back to the car. He stuck his head in further, probably looking for others.

Pretty heroic, or maybe just stupid, I thought.

The car slid further, this time shifting with a groan, as the stormy waters below hungrily lapped at it. He skipped clear to avoid being taken with it. Something shifted inside his jacket. He quit his search to hastily adjust it.

"You're by yourself?" he asked, seemingly wishing I weren't alone.

"What the fuck do you think?" I said at his nerve. "Somebody's in the trunk?"

He wiped the rain from his face, not sure what to make of me. Although winded, he tried to make amends. "Let me help you up."

"I can do it myself."

As soon as it was said, I regretted it. I tried to stand in the muddy thicket and fell again. Wet and nasty; not in a good way either. My stilettos were mired in the gunk.

He didn't laugh. Just came over. "Here."

I took his hand, strong to the touch. One of his fingers was in a splint. He gingerly held that one aside. I wondered if this was the same hand he'd used on the glass. As I rose, the car crept further down the hill, becoming wedged in some thick branches just above the river.

We both stared at it, expecting the branches to give up their catch and release it with a rousing splash. Instead, they held.

That drama averted, he led me up the hill to the relative safety of the highway. At street level, I was better able to see him beneath the lights. He was a smallish man with a round face, almost disproportionate to his body. I could imagine him once wearing glasses, or perhaps he still did. He wore nice clothes—as ruined as they were by his bravery—like some sort of businessman.

"Thank you," I offered as we walked toward what was probably his car on the side of the road. Its headlights were off, obscuring it slightly.

"Here." He removed his jacket and placed it over me. It reeked of alcohol. Even in the rain I could smell it. "Forgot your coat?" he asked.

"Yeah. I guess I left it back . . . where I was. I was in a rush."

"Rush? You could've killed someone," he scolded.

"I was trying to get somewhere. I was trying to get home."

"Not driving like that." He shook his head, chuckling at my answer. "The only place you were going was to a cemetery."

"You're not my father."

He took another look at me, beholding my scant

attire this evening. "No," he answered. "Definitely not."

I stopped in my tracks. He'd gone another few steps before noticing I wasn't beside him.

"What? Do you want to stand here in the rain? You're going to be sick in the morning."

"I don't need your shit."

"I'm not giving you any. Let's just get in my car; then you can decide what you want to do." He began walking again, never once looking back. I didn't like that.

Despite his jacket, I had begun to shiver. I didn't have a lot of body fat, and the cold was creeping into my bones. My decision reached, I ran to catch up.

He's got money, I thought, eyeing the exotic sports car as I entered the passenger side. The softness of the leather was comforting, the interior isolated. The expensive watch on his wrist jangled as he screwed the cap on a bottle of Scotch. He hurriedly threw it into what passed for a backseat, seeming embarrassed by what I'd witnessed.

"Do you have a name?"

"Henry."

"Thank you . . . again, Henry."

"You're welcome." He gazed beyond the ruined jacket, admiring my damp breasts clinging to the black satin corset they were scrunched into.

"I probably ruined your night."

"Let's just say I had plans." He broke off from his daze.

"Yeah. I can see." My eyes rolled in the direction of the half-empty bottle.

He didn't want to talk about it. "Want me to drop you off at the emergency room?"

"No. I'll be fine. A little bump on my head's not going to stop me."

"Do you want a ride somewhere then?"

I would've expected a straitlaced someone like him to offer to call the police or something. To the contrary, he wanted away from here as much as I did. Fascinating.

"Sure." I pointed seductively in the direction I would've been traveling if not for my mishap. I let my finger linger a second longer, as if the atmosphere were thick enough to play with. Truth be told, it was. "Drive."

He started his car, briskly accelerating past the busted guardrail and what lay below. A faint, rising puff of smoke was a reminder of what I would have to deal with in the morning. Or rather, what Bianca would have to deal with. It was her car, after all.

Henry's discomfort was evident as we entered Hunter's Green, "across the track" from where a man like him probably lived. His eyes darted about nervously as a red light brought our journey to a temporary halt. I imagined him wanting to run it.

At the corner, the convenience store encased in dark burglar bars was closing for the night. It was one of those kinds that sold singles, cigarettes busted out of the pack, beside lottery tickets and condoms.

"Are we close?" He was counting until his light turned green.

"No. Just keep driving. Do you have any music in here?"

"I'm not in a music mood tonight."

"Okay. Suit yourself." I removed his jacket, no longer able to tolerate the stench. A full view of my corset, the black stockings (one of them now ripped) attached to straps and garters, the formerly shiny black heels adorning my feet, gave him pause. His light turned green and he took off, but he was of split allegiances now: me and the road.

"I didn't get your name."

"I didn't give it to you." Did I even know it? My head throbbed, still hazy.

"Don't you think you should? Or do you want me to make something up?"

"Pumpkin," I answered whimsically. Clarity had arrived.

Henry's lust was put on pause by my answer. He contained his chuckle as he immediately pulled the car over. He hit the switch on his door, unlocking mine with a click.

"Look, *Pumpkin*. Contrary to how it looks, I don't have any money, so I think you got the wrong guy at most definitely the wrong time. This isn't going to be your night."

"Huh?"

"You're a working girl, right?"

"No." I hadn't fully considered how it . . . *I* looked.

"Then where were you coming from?"

"Don't worry about it. Just drive. Please."

"And I know where we're at. So, if you're thinking about setting me up and jacking me around here—"

"Oh, because you got a gun, you're all dangerous now?"

"Wha—"

"Yeah. I saw it when you pulled me out my car. I already told you. I ain't no prostitute."

"You're speeding around in *someone's* car late at night and you're dressed like that. Now we're in the middle of Hunter's Green."

"So?"

"So, I just thought . . ."

"You thought you were going to fuck me."

"What?"

"I know when a man wants to fuck me. Your tongue's been touching your shoes since I took off your jacket. Look, I'm not trying to jack you or hit you up for money. I just want to go home. Well, to my sister's place. She lives in Coventry."

"Coventry?" He knew the exclusive neighborhood we would eventually arrive at if he kept driving and quit talking. The sheer opposite of Hunter's Green, Coventry was known for its renovated buildings from the city's heyday with equally renovated money flooding in to claim it. Where crack pipes of the eighties had ruled, it was now hard to find a crack on the sidewalk. Bianca had so much going for her, but never really appreciated—or exploited—it.

I'd have to work on that.

"Yes," I answered. "Where did you think I was going? Here?"

"Well . . ."

"Don't answer that."

"Look, I'm sorry about jumping to conclusions."

"If I jumped to conclusions, I'd call you a drunk. Maybe suicidal, with that gun you're packing. How would that feel?"

"It . . . it might feel right, Pumpkin. Shit's really crazy for me."

It was several miles out of Hunter's Green before I spoke.

"Whatever you were thinking about doing . . . it's not worth it."

"Thinking?" He laughed. "You just don't know. You're acting like I'm not thinking about it anymore."

"You're not."

"Why?"

My hands traipsed up my legs, like in that nursery rhyme "The Itsy Bitsy Spider," one hypnotic step at a time across the fine mesh covering them. I undid a garter and rolled a stocking down my extended leg. When at my ankle, I brought my leg in and finished removing it. I took his hand, guiding his tensed knuckles against my bare inner thigh ever so lightly. "Because you're thinking about this," I answered.

"Uh-huh. Because you know when a man wants to fuck you?" A man attempting to be hard . . . um . . . *resistant* is a funny sight.

"*Wants?* Yes." I moved him deeper, taking his fingers past the silk of my panties and into something softer and more inviting. I began guiding him in the ways of probing and pleasing me. In and out. In. And out. His fingers had a pulse of their own, gently writhing inside. I closed my eyes, sensations overwhelming me. "And I know when a man *is* . . . going . . . to."

He stopped the car so suddenly, so violently, that I was startled. I shifted forward in my seat—tried moving, but Henry halted my progress. His hand was still doing as instructed. *Good boy.*

"You're right. I want some of that . . . bad. You're making me crazy. Let's get a room. Or go by my place."

"Maybe . . ." Climax. ". . . another time."

"No, no," he protested, desperate to get his way. "Now."

"Can't."

"Yes. You can."

"We're here."

He followed my eyes to the five stories of pristine tan brick we were parked in front of. The top three floors were my temporary home. The doorman to my sister's place had come outside, doing his job and braving the weather in his yellow windbreaker. Standing in the rain, he strained to make out our images. Henry's car was meant to attract attention, just not at this time.

"Come with me."

"Not tonight. My sister's going to be waking up soon. And I'm going to have some explaining to do about her car."

"Oh. Right." He nervously removed his hand, his fingers damp with my essence. Shit. I was about to have him eat me out to no end.

"I'll make it up to you." Was it pity or gratitude for the rescue? I don't know. I did know my promise would delay whatever rash agenda he'd been pursuing.

"Want me to come by and pick you up?"

"No. Better not." The doorman inched closer. A damn fine stud he was. "Don't need any more drama. My sister's a prissy little princess, and her husband is a controlling dick."

He laughed. "I used to work for one like that."

"Don't know how they'll handle me being around."

"I know how I would," he said, his appetite already whetted.

"I gotta run," I said, resisting the urge. I'd have time later. "Give me your number."

I waved at the doorman as Henry located a pen and a piece of paper. He waved back, still unable to discern the car's occupants. His caution abated, he returned to his post.

"Here." He placed the number in my hand. When I looked at it, he stole a kiss. I ignored the alcohol and his brashness, giving in to his surprising passion.

His tongue filled my mouth while his hands wantonly went back to their goal. With no other clothes, it wouldn't take long for him to have me totally naked.

I braced myself, giving me a moment to slow things. His kiss ended, he reverted back to form. "Aww, c'mon now!" he pleaded.

"Tomorrow," I whispered before fleeing into the building. As the doorman granted me entry, I heard the roar of Henry's car as it vanished into the night. The sentry was an amusing sight, admiring the car before realizing what he had before him.

"Um . . ." His eyes widened as two legs now claimed dominance over four wheels. "Are you okay, ma'am?"

He was cute. Real cute. "I'm fine," I said, parading into a turn. "Can't you tell?"

"No doubt," he said, slipping into his regular vernacular the building paid him to forget in front of its residents. "Do you live here?"

"Yes. Third floor. And the fourth. And the fifth."

He began choking as the realization overtook him. Probably feared losing the well-paying job. "Ma'am, I'm sorry. I didn't recognize . . ."

"My sister," I finished. "You're thinking about my sister."

"Oh." He seemed more confused than ever. It didn't hide the bulge in his ever-expanding khakis. Didn't know they were made to do that.

"I know. Honest mistake. Different hair," I said, shaking the damp out of the long strands. Bianca wishes she had this.

"Yeah," he agreed with an unusual smile. "Eyes too."

"You must *really* pay attention to Mrs. Coleman. Think she's hot, huh?"

"Yeah," he admitted with his phrase of the night. "I . . . I mean, no. Not like you."

"You're just saying that because it's late and I'm all . . . wet."

"Nah, I'm sayin' that because you're better than her. Much better."

I dragged my weary body toward the elevator. "Now, that's what I needed to hear. Good night."

He was still watching me as I entered the golden

doors. I paused before pushing the button to take me up. "What's your name?"

"Ruben." "Ma'am" was gone from his vocabulary now. He looked out into the night, wondering if anyone else would be returning late.

"Think you can keep quiet about all of this tonight?"

He licked his full lips. "Yeah."

"Good." I pushed the button to take me to the third floor. The doors responded, closing. Before they sealed completely, I pushed the button to stop them. As they reversed, Ruben sprang to attention.

"Ma'am?" he asked, not sure if formality was back in session.

I smiled seductively, leaning against the elevator's railing. "Know how to eat pussy, Ruben?"

He locked the front door, grinning as he walked over to answer my question.

Well, all right then.

3

BIANCA

*M*om is going to be mad.

I repeat it to myself over and over. Rocking and sway-
ing in the chair where my feet can't touch the floor. It's
another rainy day in Seattle. The sun's taking a nap and
I want to as well. The diner is crowded, loud. Smells of
strong coffee and sweet, sweet maple syrup jar my senses,
repulsing and attracting me. A paper turkey on the wall
reminds me of the Thanksgiving picture I drew for Mom,
but have yet to give to her.

I want to go home.

Mom is going to be mad.

My dad doesn't hear me, although he smiles and nods
as if reading my thoughts.

Soon. We'll go home soon, his face reads.

His eyes are on me, but his ear is somewhere else—
captive to the lips of someone not my mom.

Mom is going to be mad.

Rather than sitting in one of the bar chairs like me,
he stands. He likes it here. The people like him too. My

mom says they like his hair, black and curly because he has Sicilian in him. I don't know what that means. I just know it's fluffy and shiny. I wish mine would shine, but that's only when Mom puts grease in it.

My dad delivers bread in a big truck. I guess to this place too. The pretty lady behind the counter, the one with yellow hair and dirty plates in her hand, smiles as he speaks. She's amazing. I don't know how she holds all those plates.

Then she looks at me as she puts the plates down. My dad says something to her. She moves her hair, so different from mine, off her shoulders. She cracks a smile first; then I mimic her.

I think she's nice.

"Honey, wake up! Look at me."

"Huh? Why are you so loud?" I groaned. Tanner hovered over our bed, staring at me in an unusual show of concern. My head hurt and my body ached. Probably coming down with something, I thought. My PJ top wasn't even buttoned correctly, one button off at every hole. My tall husband crouched as if to scoop me up in his arms. "What's wrong?" I asked, sliding toward the center of the pillow-top mattress before he could attempt it.

"The dealership called me last night. They found your car by the river and had it towed in. I fell asleep at my desk, so I didn't get the message until now. Lorenda said you were here, so I came right home."

"Oh. That," I calmly answered. I'd begun correcting my buttons. Habit. "I'm fine. You know I never drive well in bad weather."

"Are you sure you don't need a doctor? I could have one over within the hour." He loved demonstrating his control of things. I'd seen that the day I first met him. The day he took control of my life.

"I'm fine, Tanner. Really." As his intensity subsided, I grasped his hand. He sat down beside me. "Now . . . how bad is my car?"

"The shop said it's totaled. At least it was at the end of its lease," he lamely joked. He owned the dealership—actually, several of them.

"Wait." His side of the bed was undisturbed. "You didn't come home?"

"I'm sorry. I know I promised not to do that. We've had some recent employee issues that have me pulling out my hair." His curly mane was intact, well-groomed, with just a hint of gray beginning to appear. "Besides, you were supposed to come by last night and get me."

"You're right. Well, you know how that turned out."

"You're joking. Definitely okay."

"Told you."

"Are you going by the shop today?"

My head was pounding. "No, I think the ladies around here will have to do without their shoes for one day."

20

"Good for you," he said, pretending to chuck me on the chin. "I don't like you working anyway. So, how did you get home?"

"I flagged somebody down. A nice family," I answered, not really knowing what had happened.

Tanner's fears allayed, he excused himself to shower. He would take a quick power nap, then go back to his office to crack the whip. Honestly, the man never slowed.

Tanner Coleman was a self-made millionaire. The story had appeared in so many newspapers and magazines that I could recite it from memory. After completing college at North Carolina A&T, he lucked out and inherited his grandparents' small-town fried-chicken business. In less time than he'd spent in school, he'd turned the single restaurant around, developed a blueprint, and sold franchises throughout North America. Of course, he'd diversified his holdings, investing in car dealerships and real estate to round it out. To say he was driven was an understatement. He was a man of many passions, as I'd come to learn in the five years since we'd married. Either please him or get categorized along with that which displeased him. Not somewhere you wanted to be. Me? I just wanted to be loved. I think that's all I ever wanted since getting off that Greyhound from Seattle.

Fatigued, I longed to return to bed. It was time

to get up, though. And somebody had some explaining to do.

As Tanner showered, I decided to use one of the spare baths. If I hadn't, he would probably coax me to join him in spite of what he imagined to have been my ordeal. I grabbed a towel to wash my face. As I ran my hands under the running water, I waited for it to cool, imagining what Lorenda had cooked for breakfast downstairs. A big glass of orange juice and some wheat toast would do me fine right about now.

I was startled from my thoughts by a figure in the mirror—about my same height and build, but with much longer hair and those wild, fiery eyes.

"Oh!" I shrieked. "Don't you know how to knock?"

"Did you tell him?" she blurted out before I could recover from jumping out of my skin.

"Damn it, Pumpkin! You scared the hell out of me!"

"Sorry," she meagerly offered. "Did you tell him?"

"No. And I'm not. He thinks I was driving. He doesn't know you're here, and I'm not bringing you up. Not yet, at least." I brought the cool, damp towel to my face, wishing my houseguest weren't here. "That's a touchy subject to begin with," I continued.

"I hear ya, sis. He would flip if he knew I was visiting."

"It's a big house and he's always at work, so I might get away with it."

"Always at work? That's not good." She *tsk*ed. "You must not be fucking him right."

"Pumpkin!"

"What? I'm just saying. I know how men are. Really."

"Uh-huh," I offered with a long roll of my eyes. She made me uncomfortable when she talked like this. It was that as well as her prior dealings with Tanner that left me with an ill feeling in the pit of my stomach. "Just shut up."

"I'm only looking out for you, Bianca. If you'd like, I could teach you a few . . . tricks. Blow the tall fella's mind."

"Already causing problems."

"That's not me, sis. I'm here to solve problems."

"Like my car, Pumpkin?"

She chuckled. "Oops. But you gotta admit some blame in that too. You should've never had me out there in your car in the first place. You know I don't drive worth a shit."

Pumpkin came beside me, flipping her hair and admiring herself in the mirror as I tried to finish wiping my face. She was so vain. I looked miserable and yet she looked ready for the club—her clothing way too revealing, as was her nature. "How much longer will you be here?"

"Not too long. Just long enough to take care of some things. You don't mind, do ya?"

"Do I have a choice?"

Pumpkin smirked. "No. Not really."

4

HENRY

The Scotch was releasing its hold, the corrupting genie retreating back into the bottle at the side of my bed. My broken finger ached almost as much as my throbbing head.

I awoke with questions I wasn't prepared to truthfully answer. Was I going to rob a man at gunpoint? Would I have killed him if he didn't get with the program? And did I really pull a woman from a car? A woman like *that*? Those legs, that body. The things she stirred up in me. So wild and reckless. Crack dreams. Straight-up crack dreams. One certainty was that I was out of control.

I always was a risk taker. That's why I succeeded, going beyond what was expected—my SATs in high school, summer school in college while holding down two part-times, one of which brought me to the attention of Tanner Coleman—the man. Out there on a wire was where I lived. Sometimes you fall off the wire . . . if you're lucky. Other times, the wire can be used to hang you. To the average-average on the street, things looked steady, but the eyes were slowly rolling back, a faint breath escaping my lips.

The gambling was small at first, those random long shots seeming like pure, undiluted genius. One big hit and I was caught up, ignoring the losses that piled up one after another. If only the ball would've fallen this way or that. If only that player weren't knocked out of the game with a concussion. Before I knew it, I was deep in debt, too arrogant to change my ways or lifestyle in spite of it. I kept after the elusive prize—that big payday that would right everything—but it never came. It was as if the world were conspiring to fuck me. Tanner Coleman's firing was the last hard one with no Vaseline.

Sure, I was borrowing company funds to cover a bet, but I was going to put it back. I wasn't a thief. The worrisome part was that perhaps I'd become something worse.

Thanks to somebody in the company, that was one wager that didn't get covered. And I was left without the payment I'd promised. Broken promises, just like my finger and whatever else was coming up if I didn't honor my obligations.

Worries spurred me to action. Ignoring the pain, I sat up.

Ten a.m. and *The Price Is Right* playing on my TV. The crowd was booing an old man who didn't spin the wheel all the way around. So this was what morning felt like to the unemployed. At least I could grab a bowl of cereal before planning my next move. Maybe I'd scout out Tanner again at his office—one more go-round. The clock was ticking. Someone would be calling on me later. And not Pumpkin, whom I probably would never hear from again.

I sniffed my finger for confirmation. In the dried residue, I detected faint traces of her treasured offerings. Thoughts of her were a danger akin to being out on that wire again. I should've never let her get out of my car.

A noise from my kitchen broke me from my yawn. It was a cabinet closing. This place didn't have roaches, and none of my acquaintances had a key. As poor of thought as I'd been, I knew I'd locked my door when I came in. Not sure where I'd dropped my gun or what I would do, I crept toward the sound, ready for a confrontation.

Feet resting atop my dining table as if it were a piece of furniture from the Layaway Depot, he slurped milk from my bowl. "You're out of cereal," Kash joked, as if I were still his friend from high school. He dropped the empty box onto the kitchen floor. I felt my stomach tighten, a familiar mechanism, considering the pain I equated with him. I turned and darted.

Run, was all my instincts commanded me to do.

Those instincts led me right into the fist of Lupe, his muscle, who had been silently standing behind me the whole time.

My body thumped onto the hardwood floor, where his big-ass foot came to rest on my chest. I struggled to catch my breath.

"I know, I know. I'm early. But when I didn't hear from you, I got *concerned*," Kash offered as he joined Lupe in the view from above. Both of them equally large, they were matching mounds of chocolate and vanilla. I'd known Kash since puberty, back when neither one of us was getting any action. Back then his nickname came from someone teasing about his taste for black attire, asking him one day, "Who do you think you are? Johnny Cash?" He still hung with a shady crowd, but by a simple change in the first letter and by virtue of the money now flowing through his hands courtesy of those who shared my addiction, he'd claimed the joke as his own. Kash— the man with the answer for all your vices.

"I was going to call." I tried to squirm free. Lupe noticed and pushed his white Nike deeper into my chest. I quit moving. "I've been busy trying to get your money."

He produced my gun, waving it in front of my face, daring me to grab at it. "With this? What's this about?"

"Protection," I mumbled.

"Protection," he repeated. "From what? Surely

not from us. We're your friends." Lupe grinned. Kash continued: "As good as I've been to you, Henry? Were you gonna shoot me?"

"No. How'd you get in here?" My front door didn't look busted.

He growled, "Ain't nowhere I can't go, man. Now . . . where's my money?"

"I have till tomorrow. That . . . that's what you said."

"Uh-huh. Well, it's already tomorrow somewhere in the world. You'd know that, Mr. World Traveler."

"Look . . . my watch. Take it. It's worth a couple thou."

"A couple? That watch had better be a whole lot more. You know the agreement we had."

Agreement. Interesting way of putting things.

A week ago, Kash and Lupe had caught me exiting a local Waffle House. Syrup still on my lips, the taste was smacked out of my mouth before I could get in my car. As Lupe proceeded to break my finger, we *agreed* I would make a payment toward the hundreds of thousands I owed Kash. As he knew me from back in the day, and because of the lucrative job I held, Kash told Lupe to spare my face.

The next morning I'd limped into work, finger in a splint, prepared to divert funds from Tanner's special projects fund to one I managed. The bet I was to place would've been last night.

Lupe yanked me to my feet, reminding me of the seriousness I faced this time.

"Who won last night?"

"The Cavs," Kash calmly replied. "You know LeBron don't play."

It's not fair. I would've won if I'd had that money. A sobering thought while Lupe proceeded to break the remaining fingers on my left hand. I had another extension, but the price had gone up. Something I should've been thankful for as I screamed, holding back tears. It would've been worse if they'd known that I'd lost my job.

5

BIANCA

I slowed to the curb, watching the valet as he motioned patrons forward. Even at the wheel of the new car, I shuddered over lying to Tanner. He went to great lengths to provide for me. He'd blown off the mishap, simply directing one of his dealerships to deliver something else to our place. I'd been summoned down to the lobby as if I were picking up a piece of mail. I'll never forget the look of the doorman, Ruben, as he salivated over what I thought to be a rather ordinary car. At least, that's what he told me he was looking at when I addressed the uncomfortable glances cast in my direction.

My best friend, Rory, had already arrived at the Tuscan café. From her outside table, she waved to get my attention. I lowered the window and waved back. Even before my heated discussion with Pumpkin, I was spent. I'd be sure to order some coffee once I parked.

"Mr. Clucker bought you another one, huh?"

Rory snapped between bites of her pasta salad. She never forgot the business that set Tanner on his way, even though he'd diversified, going beyond being a simple fried-chicken peddler. "What's he apologizing for this time?"

"His name is Tanner, in case you forgot. And he's not apologizing for anything. I had an accident last night."

"Oh. I'm sorry." The blond bombshell's demeanor changed. Whether through exercise, surgical means, or simply good genes, Rory Calhoun was a beautiful woman. Accustomed to men handing the world to her on a platter, she had no qualms about accepting their tribute. Most women would have found her objectionable, but she was really a sweet person once you got beyond the sculpted facade. "Are you okay? Well . . . I assume you are; otherwise you wouldn't be here."

I smiled, continuing to lie for Pumpkin. "Yes. I'm fine. Pretty radical way of getting a new car, though, wouldn't you say?"

She laughed, all the while considering whether to use the option I'd jokingly suggested. Her six-month-old baby in the stroller beside her was an unusual sight. His pacifier had him sedated for now.

"Brought Morris today, huh? He's such a cutie."

"Yeah. I figured I'd let the little monster get out. It's such a beautiful day, after all that nasty rain last night. Sometimes I wonder why I moved here."

"Where's Hazel?"

"With her nanny," she matter-of-factly replied. "Girl, you know I could only do one of them for lunch. When they get together, I can't get a word in edgewise. Isn't that right, pookie?" She'd turned to pinch her son's cheek. "Yes, yes, yes!" she cooed. Mother and son's complexions matched, with the exception of his bronze being natural while hers was sprayed on. Not enough sun around here at this time of year for her to be that brown. Both of Rory's children were biracial, the dads being professional athletes, from what I understood. With the exception of their identities, Rory didn't hide her claim to fame and how these fathers ensured that she was taken care of in exchange for keeping their names out of the news. Not my cup of tea, but I tried not being judgmental.

I summoned the waiter for another cup of coffee, feeling my eyes drooping as Rory continued to speak.

"Bianca, are you sure you're okay? You look a little worn-out."

"I'm fine. Just terribly sleepy. Don't worry. It's not the company."

"I know it isn't." She cracked a wry smile. "I take it your shop is closed."

"Yes. I was the only one on the schedule today," I said of my shoe boutique, where I carried all the latest designer brands. That was how I'd met Rory in the first place. She'd come into my establishment looking for the hottest sandals for summer during my grand opening. Even though I could've been simply the hired help, she never talked down to me. I had to let her know I was the owner when she kept trying to overtip me. We'd agreed to lunch the next day and discovered we were both from Seattle. A common bond for this girl, fresh off the bus and in a strange town, although I was sure we'd grown up on different sides of the track. And the rest, as they say, is history.

"I'm surprised Mr. Clucker even lets you work. You let that man dictate the terms of your life way too much."

I chomped down on a bite of calzone, motioning for her to wait before I replied. I was starving. Maybe that explained my lack of energy. "Tanner's not controlling," I finally offered after my last chew.

"Uh-huh. How did you meet him again?"

"Shoe store," I replied for her amusement, knowing what she was getting at. I wasn't the owner of a shoe store when I met my future husband. I was a simple sales associate trying to earn a commission. Tanner Coleman swooped in before closing with the intention of surprising his then girlfriend. The man possessed an overpowering aura, a gravity I'd never been around. In spite of his pressing mission, he asked questions, showered attention on my malnourished soul. The more he asked, the less important the shoes seemed to him. I apparently sold him more than a pair of Jimmy Choos. When I got off work, he was waiting on me. He'd called off his date on the spur of the moment. After he pleaded with me not to take the Metro back to my one-bedroom efficiency, I gave in. A whirlwind courtship ensued until I agreed to enter his world. When I used my work schedule as an excuse for some distance, he had them fire me and bought me my own boutique.

"Tanner loves me," I offered while looking at her son, Morris. He was smiling at me, clapping his hands—either a simple child doing what kids do or applause at a masterful performance.

Following lunch, I retreated to my home. The other doorman was on duty, so I was spared Ruben's peculiar interest. In the elevator mirror, I checked the dark bags forming beneath my eyes and picked at the ends of my short curls. In Seattle, I remembered the white kids' fascination over what I thought was just awkward and unruly. The black kids didn't worry about my hair. They were too busy picking at my skin color, constantly asking if my mom was white or whatever foreign notion they could conjure. Nope, just a pale, skinny black girl with confused hair from the Central District. If the society magazines in this town were to be believed, the ugly duckling had emerged a swan on the arm of Tanner Coleman.

If only emotions could be shed like feathers.

"Lorenda, I'm back," I called out as I walked into the ample expanse that was our entryway. The marble floor seemed almost glasslike, courtesy of her hard work. I set the car keys on the table and took my purse off my shoulder.

"Mrs. Coleman, I'm in here." Lorenda shouted from the kitchen. Tanner liked dinner cooked, even if he didn't come home to enjoy it.

"Anyone else here?"

There was a pause. "No. Just me and you." She hadn't run into Pumpkin yet. Good.

"Do you need anything?" she followed up.

"No. I think I'm going to bed for a while."

"Are you ill? I can bring you some medicine or some soup."

"No, I'm fine. Thank you," I replied. She was always so helpful, so motherly. I didn't know what I'd do in this place without her warm spirit.

I retreated into the master bedroom, determined to rest up for Tanner. He'd spared me his carnal demands out of concern over the car wreck.

My pass was up.

6

PUMPKIN

"**M**rs. Coleman, I knew you'd smell my soup. I . . ."

Shit.

We slammed into each other as I scurried down the hallway. Here I was trying to sneak out of my sister's prison and I ran dead into her damn maid. The bitch's eyes met mine, nervous and disapproving. Like I couldn't borrow some of Bianca's clothes. She was asleep and wouldn't mind. Besides, they fit me better. I rolled my eyes back at her and looked away. All this under-wraps stuff could drive a woman out of her ever-lovin' mind.

"Hey," I said. I rushed past her before she could ask or accuse, putting my cell to my ear in pretense to keep her at bay.

Out the lobby door (pussy-eating Ruben was off, I saw) and away from the suffocation, I pulled out my cell again, but made a call this time. I'd wait down the block for the response to my request. I smiled wickedly when the familiar sports car turned the corner an hour later. I emerged from the shelter of Starbucks, dumping my latte, and approached.

"Still alive?" I asked as I put my seat belt on. Henry was quizzical in his stare.

"Something like that," he dryly replied as he shook his head. The hand with the splint was now encased in a cast, its fingers fixed in a strange partial curl.

"Where was it you wanted to take me last night?" I smiled, waiting till it was reflected in him. He reached out with the undamaged hand and lightly touched my cheek. Tenderness wasn't something I was accustomed to. I grasped it and inserted the fingers into my mouth, applying my lips and gently sucking.

"You're crazy," he offered in faint protest.

"Maybe the world is crazy and I'm the only sane one. Want to watch old ladies cross the street, or are we going somewhere?"

He left a trail of rubber on Lancaster Boulevard as he rocketed me away, old ladies be damned.

Henry's apartment was a few tax brackets below Bianca and Tanner's, but still impressive. Deep reds and oranges defined the walls. Rich oil paintings and ornate metal sculptures that blended perfectly with the rich hardwood demonstrated his control over the domain. In spite of the initial impact, something wasn't quite right. Its current condition mirrored that of its owner. Sure, the paintings were hung right and all the furniture was in place, but the place felt as if it were a hollow space. It was missing a presence.

Noises came from Henry's bedroom. I heard him curse as he threw things around. I left the couch where he'd deposited me and investigated. This room was different from the others. Clothes lined the bed in a haphazard fashion. The bottle of Scotch from his car rested on its side, its cap missing. It was empty. This was where he lived . . . or perhaps where he hid from something, an avoidance of life.

A large duffel bag was being stuffed with shirts, pants, and jewelry.

"Running from something? Or do you have a charity you suddenly feel like donating to?"

"Just relocating. Temporarily. A couple of roaches keep turning up."

"Something to do with your situation?" I wiggled my functioning digits in the air.

He didn't answer at first. He would have scowled except he didn't have the energy. "You called me to pick you up, remember?" he retorted, zipping the duffel bag shut with his good hand. "I was in the middle of this when you called."

He turned his back to me, no longer the eager man he'd been before. I walked over, desiring physical contact, wanting him to gaze deeply into my eyes, wanting him to crave me like he had in the predawn hours.

"I'm not trying to give you grief, baby. You saved me when I needed it the most. You're my hero. I owe you."

"You don't owe me shit, Pumpkin. Forget about it." He retreated into his walk-in closet, gathering more of his life so he could run. I didn't like being ignored.

"Hello!" I shouted.

"What?" He peered from within, showing a trace of the concern he'd shown before.

"Is this how you entertain your guests?"

"I'm sorry. Once we get out of here, you'll have my full and undivided attention." He saw how the jeans fit me, how the white hoodie top clung in all the right places. I'd even borrowed some of Bianca's best perfume. He concluded after his long pause, "Uh-huh. Undivided. No doubt."

"But I don't feel like waiting." I played with the top's zipper.

"Go check out the view. It's really nice."

No, he didn't. Being here and free of Bianca's whining helplessness was better than nothing, I surmised. I resigned myself to "check out the view."

I pulled the curtain aside and took it in. I hated to admit it, but Henry was right: It was a beautiful view.

Placing a small metal box on his bed, he saw me in the window. He calmly smiled. "I used to lie in my bed on weekends and watch the park and the hills off in the distance."

Just below us, a tenant had a courtyard with his very own green space. The scholarly-looking gentleman was walking with a cup of either coffee or tea in his hand. He'd noticed my silhouette filling Henry's window as I surveyed things. He raised his cup, giving me a nod. I overdid my wave just for kicks. He nodded his head, but never took his eyes off me. *Good boy.* If only Henry were as well trained.

"Are you almost finished?" I asked, biting my lip as a devilish notion took root.

"Almost," he replied.

"Good."

I unzipped my hoodie slowly. The soft cotton top peeled away from my flesh, exposing its luscious captives. I cradled them in my hands and leaned forward. Henry's neighbor watched me intently as my warm bare breasts came in contact with the jarring cold of the windowpane. Shocked to attention, my nipples swelled. I raised a breast to my mouth, pausing to see if he'd turn away and retreat inside. He calmly sipped from his cup, standing his ground. I imagined he was aroused and playing the game. I smiled, flicking my tongue across the plump nipple. The sensations ebbed and flowed, exciting me further. I felt something stirring, my kitty purring as it awoke from its slumber.

Meow.

Henry touched my bare back with his good hand, startling me from my display.

"Forget about me?" he asked. He applied a thumb into my shoulder blade, eliciting a murmur from me. The pressure was just right. The neighbor couldn't see Henry from his vantage point.

Good.

"I thought you'd forgotten about *me*," I flipped back at him.

"And you decided to amuse yourself?"

"Uh-huh. It's hot in here. Don't you feel hot?"

"You're crazy," he whispered in my ear as he came closer. The hand was massaging my shoulder now—stronger, deeper with the pressure. He tenderly sucked on the bottom of my earlobe. I became weak-kneed.

"Uh-huh." I grunted. "Maybe."

His slacks left little to the imagination as he began to press against me from behind. Through my jeans, I tried to grip him with my ass cheeks, straddling his hard dick with every thrust. As he nibbled on my neck, I stole a glance out the window. Henry's neighbor had finished whatever he was drinking. The cup dangled in his hand. He could see I wasn't alone anymore, yet stayed the course.

"Come here." Henry snatched me off my feet,

intent on bringing me to his bed. The high-thread-count sheets would've felt good on my body, but I declined. This was too much fun. I begged him to put me down.

"No." I turned my back to the voyeur and began to exit my jeans and panties. I gyrated sensually as I took them off, giving him a show from the rear while Henry was captivated by my front.

"You're so beautiful," he muttered, pleased with my dance. "Is this real?"

"It looks real to me." I backed my ass cheeks against the glass, feeling the cold chill that had delighted my breasts. I spread my legs, extending a Brazilian-waxed invitation I knew he'd RSVP to. "How does it look to you?"

His reply was a drop of his slacks, that mighty dick of his fully visible for me to see. My eyes lit with delight. He got his shirt unbuttoned and halfway off before getting it snagged on his cast. There it stayed, as I wouldn't be put off a minute longer. As Henry entered me from the front, I imagined the man below as if he were in the room with us, wanting a piece of me as I knew he did. I thought of him joining in, removing his pants, and penetrating my awaiting ass. The thought of being sandwiched between two hungry, frenzied males made me cum and convulse even more. I writhed greedily as Henry filled my moist cavern, driving to that point when a man becomes a baby again.

"Harder," I urged in his ear as I held him tightly. "That's it. Umm . . . umm. Mmm-hmmm. Gawd, you feel so good, Henry. That's it."

Henry's passion made me forget the imaginary company in the room with us. He fucked me like his life depended on it, pushing me farther up the window frame with each torrid thrust. I came again and wept uncontrollably, satisfied on so many levels with his effort.

The sweet stickiness forming between our bodies was intoxicating. I clung to him, burying his face in my breasts for a taste.

"Oh, this is so good."

"Ain't it, though?" I panted. "C'mon. Pumpkin's got what you need. Go ahead and get it, baby."

Henry flexed and drove deeper into me, determined to throw my back out. As I banged against the firm glass again, I cast an outward glance. The neighbor was still there. His cup had fallen to the ground. That hand had another agenda at the moment as he sought some sort of participation in our encounter. Poor man. He'd come outside for a "spot of tea" or something and would be leaving with a spot on his pants.

Hitting *my* spot, Henry usurped my attention with his final push. In such a short time, he'd learned to play my body like an instrument. I'd originally planned on offering the pussy as a reward for what he'd done. Now? Now, I was thinking this might be kind of fun over the long haul. He sent shudders through my spine as he erupted. After several lovely orgasms, my journey was over.

Yes, indeed.

I tried sneaking back into Bianca's place. Her clothes would have to be washed before she threw a fit and started questioning me like she was my mom or something.

"How was your day?" the damn maid asked, looking at me strangely. It was as if she'd been waiting for me. Didn't she ever go home?

I held up a hand, telling her I wasn't in a chatty mood. After a fucking like I'd received, I didn't need her bringing me down.

"Bitch has to go," I thought aloud, not caring if she heard. She was cramping my style. And I would have to do something about that. Best believe.

7

HENRY

As I slumped against Pumpkin, it took all I had not to fall over. We were pressed together in my windowsill, our labored breathing in a heated race. It was as good as I had imagined. Success had improved my odds with women over the years, allowing me to pick and choose some of the finest. Even then, it was according to a formula. If I went to a certain place to eat or a certain event, there always was a certain type of woman I could get with based on my finances or how I dressed or what I drove. Pumpkin didn't fit into a formula. She had the wild, unrestrained nature a brother would usually pay for, but hidden below was someone much deeper than that. Don't ask me how I knew it so quickly. Like I said, I knew risk and reward. Maybe she was my good luck charm, something guiding me to a big winning streak in life.

Finally prying myself away, I dared to exhale. My shirt still dangled on my arm, caught on my messed-up hand. Eyes adjusting to the light outside my window, I saw Mr. Reyes in his courtyard. As I focused, he realized I was looking at him. He hastily went inside, kicking his cup aside as he departed.

Pumpkin had begun to stir and was breathing a long sigh.

"Did you see him?" I asked.

"Who?" she answered as she stepped over the clothes she'd shed. Her toned, long legs cleared them easily. I fixed on her round ass as she continued to my crowded bed. She bent over, pushing the accumulation to the floor without a care.

"My neighbor," I replied as she continued clearing. She didn't care about the view I had. "He was outside. Down there. While we . . ."

Dazzling eyes suddenly looked devilish. With a turn of her head, she swished the strands of long black hair clear of her light brown skin. "Oh. Him. Don't worry about that," she said smartly. "Come lie down with me."

I started to remind her of my original mission, of why I was packing. Looking at my bag and other stuff discarded on the floor, I realized it was pointless. Besides, my fingers had earned me another extension with Kash. As good as it was, another taste of my good-luck charm couldn't be a bad thing. She motioned for me to come. Feeling the advent of another hard-on, I forgot about the man outside my window and my current dilemma.

. . .

"Do they hurt?"

"Only when I laugh." I groaned.

At a time when I wanted to catch a quick nap or maybe cuddle with the figment in my arms, she was wide awake. If it weren't rude, I would've turned my back to her. Either this woman was wired or she was afraid of sleeping. She climbed atop me, demanding my attention.

"Truth time," she said, poking me in my chest, where she'd recently left passion marks.

"Oh, Lord."

"Talk. Who's been snacking on your fingers? You owe somebody some money? Stole something?"

When I was about to blow her off, her deductions let me know she wasn't one to take for granted. My frivolous attitude ended. "Damn. You're good," I remarked.

"Just good at figuring shit out. If you owe something, they probably would've killed you."

"I'm sure that's a possibility."

She dropped the know-it-all smile. "That's why you're packing?"

"Bingo."

"How much are you on the hook for?"

"Change the subject."

"No. You could've left me for dead on the side

of the road, but you didn't. You helped me, Henry. Now I want to help you."

Those eyes, those beautiful eyes. Full of truth, yet so full of mystery.

"You can't help me."

"How do you know if you don't ask?"

"What do you want me to do? Ask you for help?"

"That would be a start."

"Okay," I said, humoring her. "Help me, Pumpkin."

"That's better," she purred. She got off me, allowing me to sit up. "Now, how much do you need?"

"I'm not going there with this."

She shook me. "Answer me, Henry."

"I need twenty-five thousand right now."

"But that's not all you owe."

"No. That's just to get me an extension. It wasn't that large in the beginning. Interest and 'late fees' kept getting added on. I had something in the works, but lost my job the other day."

Pumpkin sighed. I was expecting her to put on her clothes and walk out the door. She didn't move. "Is that why you had that gun last night?"

I nodded.

She looked at me strangely, which made me uneasy for some reason. "You got fired? Where did you work?"

"At that building where you were last night." I

regretted letting that slip the moment it left my lips. I was exhausted, careless.

"Huh? Were you following me?"

I stared her dead in the eyes, fearful of letting anyone know just how desperate I was. "No. I was traveling behind you. That's all." Since we were on the subject, I figured I'd ask some questions of my own. Just for my own peace of mind. "I used to work for Tanner Coleman. Ever hear of him?"

"No," she answered. I didn't detect any deceit. Good. Like I figured, she'd probably been visiting someone on another floor in the building last night for whatever reason. "Should I know him?" she followed up.

"Naw. Just an asshole who thinks he runs this town."

Her laugh was unsettling. "Don't do anything rash, Henry. I'll see what I can do for you. After all, one good turn deserves another."

A good-luck charm she might turn out to be, I thought.

8

BIANCA

"**G**o to bed, princess," my dad says as he comes up the staircase. Ours is an older house, the bottom lived in by an Asian couple that refuses to move from the neighborhood. That's what my mom tells me when I ask why they're different from everyone else. I see people like them when my dad takes me to Chinatown. They're very nice.

"I don't want to go to bed." I pout. It's cold outside . . . again. I feel the chill as it whistles up the stairwell from the open door below. I can't see very well because the lightbulb is out again. I smell my dad's leather coat before he's taken two steps. It's my favorite. Sometimes he lets me wear it. It's too big for me, but I don't care. My mom and dad laugh when I put it on.

He stops, doesn't take another step. I wonder what's wrong. Is my dad hurt? "Go give your mom a kiss; then go to bed," he urges.

I ignore what he says and run to him instead. I almost fall because I can't see the big stairs. Then I stop. In the faint light from the street, I see he's not alone.

I don't want to go to bed.

My body shook. A quick jolt in the midst of the haze I'd awakened to.

In my bed.

Now.

Then another.

My body trembled and jerked as I tried to fight the sensations overcoming me. I had no will.

"Mmmm," he moaned as he feasted in the dark. "Baby, you awake now?"

Had I slept the whole day away? I last remembered coming home after lunch with Rory.

"Huh? What are you doing?" I asked of Tanner in a barely audible whisper. My husband's face disappeared between my thighs as he took another taste of my latest orgasmic concoction. I felt his stiff tongue as it probed my clit, giving me involuntary shudders. I was tired, not feeling good, and not in the mood for him to be simply taking my stuff. I tried moving, forcing him from between my legs, but I was too weak—muscles failing from all the trembling he was bringing about. I pressed against his forehead with my palm, begging him to put this off to another night. His reply was to stick his face deeper into my pussy, licking and sucking on my swollen clit as I came against my will while subject only to his. No surprise; I never was a match for Tanner. When he wanted something, there wasn't a way to say no in any language known to man.

I gave up the fight like so many times before and let him finish his "Bianca pie," as he liked to call it. Rory never called me Tanner's slave, but I guess in so many ways, it didn't have to be said.

When his neck began cramping, the distinguished Mr. Coleman rose up, positioning me to receive his hard dick. I grimaced as he entered, sensitive from his oral feast, I guessed. He hated when I didn't cooperate or generate enough moans for his pleasure. This wouldn't take long tonight, pleasing me in some fashion. After sliding in and out of me several times, he exploded—a release from the pressures of his stress-filled world.

He would be talking about it soon, giving me all the details as his faithful confidante.

"Are you sure you're okay?" he asked while removing himself from me. He didn't look at me long. He had taken notice of several more gray hairs atop his scalp, examining them from a distance in the mirror on the wall. I think he was worried about that point when "distinguished" just started to look like "old."

"I'm sure, Tanner."

He made note of the additional grays, then moved on. "I've never known you to sleep like this. Maybe you should go to the doctor . . . make sure the car wreck didn't do anything."

"I told you I'm fine. Shit," I muttered uncharacteristically.

He frowned, hating when I cursed . . . at least in these situations. "Mad about tonight? I hope you're not. It's just that you're so beautiful and irresistible. You just bring it out in me." From the role-playing that began shortly after we were wed to the more exotic demands of late, I doubted that I was simply "bringing it out" in him.

"No," I said as I looked at him. "You're a man and you have needs."

"Good. I'd never do anything to hurt you, Bianca. You're my heart. It's just that things have been so crazy at work."

He paused, wanting me to egg him on. I didn't. I just wanted to get cleaned up and go back to sleep. He'd continue anyway.

"We've been going through the books." Bingo. "You know I had to fire someone for messing with my money?"

I still didn't react.

"*Our* money," he added, correcting himself to make me a part of the equation. "I'm lucky I caught the lowlife. And he'd better not try seeking a reference. Shit. He might want to move to another town, as far as I'm concerned. I have a low tolerance for thieves."

Somewhere in the monologue, I mentally wandered off. I was still hoping Pumpkin was keeping quiet and out of sight. Tanner had strict rules for having her around.

After venting, he watched some business news on CNBC before taking me to shower with him. A good idea, as I thought the steam would reinvigorate me. My aching muscles seemed to soak it up, feeling looser than they had in days. I'm not quite sure where all my tension was coming from.

We took turns soaping each other while kissing under the pulsating streams of water. Times like this were when the man I'd fallen in love with shone through. Sure, he had issues, but no couples were perfect. Maybe I was the one with issues, never up to par with this extreme alpha male whom fate had paired me with.

"How was your lunch with Rory?" he asked as I scrubbed his back with the sponge. I was over being surprised by how much he knew. Lorenda probably told him when he came home from work.

"Good," I replied as I let the nozzle rinse away the suds. "I got to see Morris, her little boy. She rarely brings him out."

"Probably doesn't know who the father is," he derided. Rory was one he disapproved of, probably because she refused to fawn over him like the rest of this town.

"That's not nice. She does know who the father is."

"Oh, really?" he said, turning around to face me. It was his turn to finish soaping me. "Did she tell you?"

"Well . . . no. I don't ask those things. But I'm sure she knows."

He laughed—hearty and full of amusement. "Probably has one of those ballplayers conned."

"Will you leave my friends alone?" I said, raising my voice. "I don't talk about yours, so . . ."

"Bianca?"

"So . . ." I couldn't finish my sentence because I was too busy trying to focus. The world had begun spinning. Maybe the hot steam was too much, too soon. I braced myself in time for Tanner to catch me. He turned off the water and opened the shower door.

"I'm fine, really." A deep breath seemed to do me some good after the near–fainting spell. I tried it again to make sure I was going to be all right. "Something just passed over me."

"Let's get you to bed. I'll call the doctor in the morning. A checkup wouldn't hurt. Can't afford a sick wife." I sounded more like a business asset than a wife with that closing remark, but took no offense.

After toweling me off, he carried me in his arms, tucking me in beneath the down comforter. Tanner then donned his PJ bottoms. His physique was still admirable and, truth be told, satisfied me when I was in the mood.

"Where are you going?" I asked as he headed toward the bedroom door.

"Eat some of Lorenda's soup, then do a little work in my office. I'll check on you in a little bit."

I nodded, beginning to close my eyes for departure.

"Baby?"

"Yes."

"You're not pregnant, are you?"

"Ha, ha," I answered, remembering the issues of his sperm count he'd told me about. I threw one of the smaller pillows in his direction. "If I were, then it wouldn't be from you. Go do some work or *something*."

"I'd rather be doing you," he joked, except I knew it wasn't a joke. Maybe if I fell asleep right now, he wouldn't bother me until morning.

On that thought I shut my eyes tightly, turning off the lights with the remote.

9

PUMPKIN

I'd come to visit and was going to get the most out of it. Lorenda the maid, who I was now contemplating calling "Horrenda," was gone for the night, and Bianca was sound asleep. I think I even heard a snore. It was best that way for her—nothing asked, nothing demanded. She barely lived her life. If I had this, I'd rule it all. Envy aside, I crept into her closet to check on something. There it was, right where I figured it would be. I zipped her purse back, then returned it to its resting place.

As I crept around, I passed Tanner's office. The man of the house wasn't to be found. A quick stop to put up what was in my hand and then I went searching for trouble.

Trouble by the name of another T was found shooting pool in the game room. The room was enveloped in darkness with only the recessed lights above to illuminate his diversion. He was listening to Sting while ingesting Scotch like Henry's, except in much smaller quantities.

Henry. Maybe I shouldn't have lied to him about Tanner. But my life was none of his business. Besides, he'd thank me for it later.

Crack.

The balls bounced around the table, subject to the calculations Tanner had made prior to taking his shot. As the last one fell into a pocket, he backed away from the table. He sipped from his glass while holding the stick, satisfied with his work.

"If you play by yourself, how do you know who won?"

He almost spilled his drink. He'd thought he was alone—alone with his smugness.

"Miss me, baby?" I asked, not fully in view.

Tanner's brow furrowed as I revealed more of myself. In the light, the olive dress and tan peep-toe slingbacks shone. I struck a pose, having fun at his expense with my features still obscured. "Like it?"

"What are you doing up?" he asked. I came closer, completely revealed. He recognized the dress and shoes to be his wife's, but now saw the shoulder-length straight hair, not his wife's. I smirked, eyes twinkling with fire.

"You?"

"Hello, Tanner."

"What are you doing? I didn't send for you."

"No. Not this time. I came for a visit on my own.

I don't take instruction very well these days. Just like the other night at your office."

He frowned, completing my thought. "When you didn't show up."

"Oops. Shit happens." I shrugged.

"You owe me for that car."

I laughed. It was nice of Bianca to try to cover for me. Tanner thought he knew what was going on. But just like his demure wife, he was ultimately clueless. "Okay, so I wrecked your dumpy car. Now, are you going to make me pay?"

He never could hold it back when I was around. His firm chest rippled as he choked up on the pool stick. Lesser wood and it would've snapped. A hard-on formed so quickly in his tidy little PJs that he probably hurt himself.

I came up to Tanner, allowing him to touch me and know the woman he really craved was here. He reached out, grabbing my hair.

"Come here," he said as he pulled me toward him for a kiss.

"Watch the hair," I said, slapping his hand. He blinked in disbelief. "I thought I'd told you about that."

"Why are you here then?"

"I want to learn how to play. Will you teach me, Tanner?"

I had to tug on his stick—pool stick—twice before he relinquished. At the table, I held the stick like I thought it went and bent over. The cotton fabric of the dress saddled up my hips. I slid the stick back, preparing for my attempt.

"No. Not like that." He was upon me, his voice steady and even. He placed his hand over mine, positioning the stick properly. "There. Now ease up on the cue. It's all about grip, stance, and aiming."

"How am I doing?"

"Better." His scholarly approach was betrayed by a roving hand. It slid down from the small of my back over the slope of my hips. His expert fingers gripped, reminding me of how much I missed a massage to the booty. With each palmful he took of my ass, the fabric's edge slowly crept up. When the soft suppleness stood revealed, he paused.

"Took you long enough," I joked as he finally noticed I wasn't wearing any panties. I took my shot, splitting the two balls like an expert. I didn't need a coach when it came to busting balls. That talent came naturally.

Unlike Tanner, I wouldn't get a moment to savor the success.

I dropped the stick, sprawling over the table as Tanner suddenly fell to his knees. He was behind me, holding me by the hips as my face rested on the long green felt before me. I gasped as he bit me on my ass.

"Ouch. Bite that shit harder," I urged. The big freak obliged.

"This what you want?"

"Oh, you know I do," I said, trying to sound more in control than he as he took another bite of the apple. I came this time. It was a juicy apple.

From the backs of my knees, he began licking up each thigh, stopping at the curve of the cheeks to nip at them. I'd begun breathing heavily in anticipation and shook my apple tree to further tantalize him. *Slap, slap, slap,* they went to a controlled rhythm.

He spread my ass cheeks and dug in, licking me from my clit up to my asshole and back again. In the middle of each journey, he'd pause to stimulate the area in between with the tip of his tongue, giving me goose bumps and making me convulse with every stab. I said he was a freak, but a freak who knows what he's doing ain't all that bad. As he continued probing and teasing, I dug my nails into the table, clawing with every climax. His thumb pressed into my asshole, pressuring to enter, as he lapped at the juices flowing onto my clit. With each venture inside my puckering muscle, I flowed harder. And he drank harder. Like a sailor who couldn't get his fill.

Intoxicated with pussy on the breath, Tanner rolled me over for the main course. This . . . this was the true face of the man who'd married Bianca. A visage smeared with my essence instead.

"You are so beautiful," he panted. He dropped his PJs for his dick to greet me. "I've missed you."

"And you talk too much." I looked at his waiting dick. "Fuck me."

Tanner slid me to the center of the pool table where the workaholic climbed atop to put in overtime on my pussy. As he rode me hard, I held back screams for fear of waking Bianca.

Grip.

Stance.

Aim.

Then the stroke to close the deal.

Yeah. We'd worked on all of those tonight. I was learning the game.

10

BIANCA

After seeing the bags under my eyes, I knew the night had been another restless one. I awoke in the afternoon feeling worse than when I'd gone to bed. Tanner's urges took their toll on a body. At least he'd spared me this morning—only a kiss planted on my forehead before he headed to the office or meetings with his attorneys. He couldn't have been satisfied with just that. To make up for it, I probably was going to be dragged to a swingers' club to watch other couples get their freak on.

"It says here you were involved in a motor vehicle accident?" Dr. Gardner asked, reading from his notes. I sat there in the hospital gown, legs locked together like they were Krazy Glued. Tanner had called in the appointment, so I had to go along with it.

"No. That's a mistake."

The balding, roundish man of fifty squinted. "Are you sure? Because it says here . . ."

I held out my hand, stopping him. "I wasn't in an accident. I was covering for a relative."

"Oh. I see," he said as he lowered the notes from his gaze. "So, why are you here?"

"I've just felt run-down . . . dizzy. I've been sleeping, but it hasn't been restful."

"Maybe you should take vitamins," he observed, curiously intrigued by the dark circles under my eyes. With my fair skin, they were easily visible. "Any changes in your routine? Any unusual stress?"

"If you mean having an unwanted houseguest, then the answer is yes."

"We've all had those from time to time. I could tell you stories about my mother-in-law," he joked. "Well, let's get you checked out. We can't have the wife of Tanner Coleman not knowing what's wrong with her. He might take away that grant for the children's wing."

And there he was in the room with us, his looming presence felt all the more during the exam.

"Are you and your husband regularly active?" Great question to ask with my feet up in the stirrups. As much as Tanner had been down there, he was vying for Dr. Gardner's job.

"Yes." I flinched, tender to the touch.

"Any discomfort or discharge?"

"No. Um . . . just a little tender." I gave a nervous laugh, the one that said to leave it alone.

"Sorry. I'll try to go easy," he said, preparing me for the Pap smear.

After the pelvic exam, he had a series of tests run, including a pregnancy test due to the dizziness. He'd ruled out mononucleosis and my being anemic, so I began to wonder if the blood tests were really about checking for STDs. I knew better than to think Tanner's lust was limited to me; I just hoped he'd respected me enough to use protection. The tests were pending, but as far as he could tell, I was okay. Just advised to take it easy—in and out of bed—and to get on some vitamins. He also prescribed something to help with my sleep. I would be sure to take that.

On the way to my boutique, I passed a billboard for Southwest Airlines. Their slogan, "Wanna Get Away?" was never more appropriate. Maybe a little vacation getaway was what I really needed. On a moment's notice, I could be jetting to Mexico or anywhere with beautiful waters and shimmering sand. Besides, I could use some work on my tan. Then I caught myself.

Not while Pumpkin was here. Just a delusion on my part.

"Bianca, are you sure these came from Italy? I could've sworn it was Portugal or one of those other countries." One of my big shoppers, as well as one of the most contentious, sipped from her flute of champagne.

"I'm sure, Mrs. Jones. You're getting these mixed up with the sandals I showed you *last week*."

"You know . . ." She paused, her eyes suddenly alert. "I think you're right." *Duh. No shit.* I smiled, leaving my thoughts to myself.

"I'll take both pairs," she squealed. "And another glass of this exquisite champagne!"

I motioned to Deonté, my assistant, to oblige the giddy Mrs. Jones with a refill. Deonté was a student I mentored as part of the community college's young-entrepreneur program. I loved her inquisitive mind and how she always questioned the status quo. She hated indulging certain customers, but understood the purpose. People came for an experience, not just a purchase. Things like that allowed one to charge a premium. That reflection made me think about my situation. Had Tanner made a purchase with me while still searching for an experience? Another big sale under my belt, I scuttled those doubts and left to retrieve the Portuguese sandals from last week.

Deonté chuckled after Mrs. Jones was gone with her shoes.

"What's so funny?"

"This whole thing. I'm from HG—Hunter's Green. I didn't come up in a world like this. Every now and then I either have to laugh, cry, or pinch myself."

"I didn't come up in this world either, Deonté," I assured her. "At times, I still feel like I'm in a fairy tale too. Sure, my husband bought this boutique for me, but deep down, I don't think he ever thought I would succeed. I put my heart and soul into it, because it's something I can claim as my own—a product of my own success, not the illustrious Coleman name. Every day I exceed his expectations is another day I hope he looks at me as an equal."

"Instead of the trophy wife?"

I glared at Deonté, a reflex to her brashness. "Maybe," I offered.

My cell phone rang at the perfect time. Two rings later, I answered.

"Mrs. Coleman?"

"Yes, this is she."

"This is Mr. Ennis from Fidelity Trust," the accommodating voice said. It was our bank. "I'm glad I was able to reach you."

"Why? Is something wrong?" Two women had entered with shoes on their mind. I motioned to Deonté to take care of them. She quickly filled two flutes with complimentary champagne and walked over. I turned my attention back to the call.

"No, no. Nothing's wrong. Our Coventry branch had a transaction this morning that we just needed to confirm."

"Oh? What transaction?"

"On your business account, ma'am. A check was

written to 'cash,' and with such large amounts, we just like to follow up for confirmation. In case something was amiss. Our records show that you and Mr. Coleman usually do wire transfers, so this seemed a little unusual."

"What are you talking about?"

"The check you cashed this morning, Mrs. Coleman . . . In the amount of ninety thousand dollars."

I wanted to drop the phone.

11

HENRY

When I received the blocked call, I hesitated to answer. Kash didn't need to know where I was holed up. I had a little time left, but I needed to think of something. The little cash I had to myself wouldn't hold out much longer. I'd failed to kill myself, and no references were coming from Coleman, I was sure.

When it rang again, I steeled myself. I debated over whether to grovel or be a man before Kash. I'd decided to be a man when I answered.

"Yeah."

"I need you to meet me," she said. I remembered to stow the man for my next encounter with Kash.

I walked off the street, expecting to see a familiar Pumpkin somewhere in the Dunkin' Donuts on Turner Avenue. A woman in a dark green business suit was sitting at a corner table playing with a cup of coffee. She lowered the designer shades to give me a familiar wink. A snazzy designer hat concealed the familiar long strands I was becoming fond of.

"Day job?" I asked.

"Don't fuck with me, Henry." She radiated irksomeness. Not my doing. I hadn't been there long enough to piss her off.

"You're the one who called. And here I go jumping again. You could at least be cordial."

"You're right," she admitted. "These clothes have me irritated. I don't like wearing this kind of shit."

"Then why did you? I could think of some things I'd rather see you in."

"I got something for that, but try putting your dick on hold for a second."

"Okay. I've been considering whether to ask you something anyway."

She ditched the shades. Her eyebrows rose in intrigue. In the light of the doughnut shop, I wondered if those brilliant eyes were the product of colored contacts. Didn't really matter. The fire that burned in them wasn't a fantasy. "I'm listening, Henry. Go for it."

I took a great big swallow of pride before pushing forward. "Remember when you said you're staying with your sister and her husband?"

"Duh. Of course."

"I was kind of fucked-up that night. Shit on my mind. But I couldn't help but notice . . ." I broke my gaze, embarrassed. "I don't know what your brother-in-law does, and you don't know all my qualifications, but I'm versatile . . . and hungry. I was wondering if you could maybe put in a word with him for me."

Pumpkin gave me the strangest look. I couldn't tell whether she wanted to burst out laughing or slap me. It faded, replaced by an unsettling pause. "I doubt it," she said. "But I do want to help you. Remember?"

"Yes. I remember what you said." I tried hiding my disappointment, preparing for whatever was to come.

She bumped my leg. I thought nothing of it until she kicked me. That warranted my looking down. I gazed upon an orange backpack placed beneath the table.

"What?" I said, looking back at Pumpkin.

"Take it with you to the bathroom. And try acting normal."

"What is it?"

"Boy, just go to the bathroom. Please." She seemed anxious.

"Holy shit!" I blurted from the toilet stall. The stacks of bills were easily over twenty thousand. I zipped the bag back, ideas swirling through my head as I tried to figure where it came from and how she got it.

When I returned, Pumpkin was standing. She

no longer feigned interest in the coffee cup. "You like?" she said.

"Yes," I gushed. "But—"

She cut me off. "I just hope that helps."

"Where did you get this?"

"My brother-in-law. Owed me a favor."

"Wait, wait. He's not a drug dealer or something?"

"No. He just deals." She found something cute in that.

I lowered the stuffed backpack, debating over whether I could take so much money. It would keep Kash at bay from the good hand with which I held the bag. It also could be rolled over into something serious . . . with the right bet or two.

"I can't take this." Better to rid myself of it before that familiar rush had reasserted itself.

Pumpkin refused to take it; just looked at me stupidly. "Why not? Because of your pride?"

"I can't pay this back," I mumbled. The man behind the counter was becoming curious. I watched his eyes as he fetched a bagel for a customer.

"I never asked you to. Just being a friend, Henry." She folded her arms.

"Let's go somewhere else, talk about this. I'm staying at a hotel across town."

"I would love nothing better than some behind-closed-doors action with you," she teased. "But I can't right now. Just take it and I'll call you later."

I said nothing, neither accepting nor refusing her gift. Just felt her kiss before she dumped her untouched coffee and darted out the door into traffic.

And I was left literally holding the bag.

12

BIANCA

I had been dealing with this branch of Fidelity Trust since my marriage. Tanner had been dealing with them way longer. When I walked into the lobby, everyone sprang to attention, smiles and mentions of "Mrs. Coleman" echoing through the halls of the century-old establishment. Not like the indifference shown me and my mom when she used to make deposits at the sterile little bank in Seattle. Whereas I was unseen and unheard before the Coleman name, now my whisper was like a roar. It amused me as much as it disturbed me.

The branch manager, Mr. Guzman, came out from behind his desk and motioned me over. He'd obviously been called and warned I was on my way. I altered my course and went straight to him. As he shook my hand, he welcomed me inside his office. Once I was seated, he closed the door. As he moved back to the other side of his desk, he went into whatever opening he'd prepared.

"Mrs. Coleman, good to see you again. I heard there was a misunderstanding?"

"Yes. If you call somebody walking in here, forging my name on a check for almost a hundred thousand dollars, and your letting them walk out that door, then there has definitely been a misunderstanding."

Guzman smiled as if he were about to laugh. He saw a joke in there. I didn't see anything funny. He quickly corrected his expression.

"Ma'am?"

"What are you doing about this? Have you called the police? Or do I need to call my husband to get some results?"

"Ma'am, please calm down. I honestly thought this was some kind of test."

"I've had an extremely difficult day. Explain. Now."

"You came in and withdrew the money yourself. I met with you."

"No, you didn't."

Now he looked nervous. "Yes. I did." He blinked, a tiny bit of doubt dissolving his swagger. "Well . . . I knew it was you. Even with the hat and sunglasses. We had a lovely conversation just like always. I thought it was a little dangerous, your leaving here with all that cash, but you convinced me it was all right. I kind of wondered why you changed before coming back."

Fear trickled into my throat. A picture was beginning to form. "I wasn't here."

"If . . . if you'd like, I can produce the check. Let you verify the signature."

While he secured the check, I sat and simmered. When he returned, he presented a check from my business account. The signature was pretty close to mine. Damn Pumpkin. She knew me too well. Better than I knew myself in some instances. I'd been pushed beyond my overly generous limits this time. And she would learn a few new things.

"Is there a problem, Mrs. Coleman?"

"No," I offered apologetically. He must've thought me mental. "Sorry to take up your time."

I scoured the house looking for her. Lorenda was all in a panic over my mood, but I told her to get out of the way. It wasn't till my bedroom that I heard signs of life.

"Is something wrong, Mrs. Coleman? Do you need me to call Mr. Coleman?"

I paused, listening to the sounds behind my door. Someone was in there.

"What? The television?" Lorenda remarked. "I'm sorry I left it on. I was cleaning in there."

It wasn't the TV I was listening to. It was the laughter in response to the television. "It's okay,

Lorenda. I have to take care of something." She stood there, confused and trying to hear what I heard. "You can go now."

I rushed into my room, not quite sure what I would see.

"What's up, Bianca?" Pumpkin calmly asked as she lay across my bed. In a pair of designer jeans and a yellow T-shirt, she rested barefoot, sporting a fresh pedicure. "I don't have a TV in my room."

I grabbed her by the leg and pulled.

"What the fuck is wrong with you?"

"Come here!" I screamed as she tried to kick my hand off her.

There was a faint tapping on the door. "Mrs. Coleman?" Lorenda's muffled voice called out in distress.

"I'm fine, Lorenda! Go away!"

Pumpkin laughed, causing me to hurl myself across the bed to slap her. She rolled away to the other side, where she sprang to her feet.

"What the fuck is wrong with you?" she screamed, holding her face in shock. *If looks could kill.* I'm sure I matched that look, though.

"Are you trying to ruin my life? Huh? Is that what you're trying to do?"

"Must be crying over my withdrawal."

"Hell, yes. I'm not crying, but I'm so angry that I could," I barked. "You're lucky I'm letting you stay here."

"Lucky? Like you have a choice now," she mouthed off. "I'm getting used to a *lot* of things around here." Her eyes cast that twisted glance, their sick taunt understood.

I jumped across the bed, causing her to run to the other side. "You bitch!"

"Watch the mouth, Bianca. Or I might stop looking out for you," she teased as she ducked my wild swings. Back on my feet, I overtook her as she scampered around the room. We banged into the furniture, sending a set of candles tumbling onto the carpet. I kicked a candleholder as we tangled, stinging my foot.

Pumpkin tried to break free again, but I'd twisted her arm. She winced in pain. Knowing Lorenda was probably camped outside the bedroom door, I pulled my sister into my walk-in closet.

"Let go of me!" I obliged as I barred any chance of escape.

"Why did you go into my purse? Huh? I'm letting you stay here and you steal from me? Me? What kind of sick bitch are you, Pumpkin?"

She folded her arms, a crazy calm in contrast to my hyped state. She pushed some of my clothes on the rack. Made me wonder how much time she'd been spending going through my things. "The kind who does everything you won't do. The kind whom you *wish* you were."

"Why are you so determined to ruin my life?"

"You don't have a life!" she screamed. "I'm just trying to show you that."

I raised my hand to slap her again.

"Do it. I dare you. Hell, I might even like it. You know I have a high tolerance for pain. Besides, you need me more than I need you."

"What did you do with the money?"

"You don't want to know. Just leave it alone."

"How can I? You robbed me! If Tanner finds out . . ."

"Tanner! Tanner! Tanner! Always worrying the fuck about Tanner. That man's got more money than he knows what to do with. I figure the little bit I took is the least he owes you."

"How do you know what Tanner 'owes' me? And why are you always so down on my husband?"

"Because he's always down on you, bitch. What you think?" she snapped, sucking her teeth. I shook my head, wanting to shake her some more. She just fixed her hair in defiance. "What? Are we done here? Because this closet is getting stuffy."

"No, we're not done. And I'm not letting you out of here until you come up with the money."

"Sure you can stop me?" She got in my face. I usually couldn't stand looking at her for an extended period of time. This time I did. Almost a mirror image, excluding those fiery eyes and hair, I grudgingly noted. No wonder Mr. Guzman at the bank was fooled. Pumpkin's smile seemed to grow to epic proportions, then suddenly blurred. I blinked a few times, but it didn't help. She was right: The closet was getting stuffy. It was hard to breathe. I took a step toward her, then stumbled slightly, another dizzy spell coming on. *Shit.* I hadn't listened to the doctor. All the stress had taken its toll.

"You look like shit, Bianca," Pumpkin teased as my head tipped back, giving me a glimpse of the closet lights before I crashed to the floor, unconscious.

13

PUMPKIN

"**M**rs. Coleman! Mrs. Coleman!" her nagging maid repeated.

Bianca looked worn-out. Poor thing was being run ragged. All she needed was a blanket and a pillow. I left her there, stepping over her to handle some business.

By the time I'd opened the bedroom door, Lorenda had moved on. Just an empty hallway stood before me.

"No time like the present," I muttered as I set out on my mission.

Lorenda was bending over her oven, checking on the roast she was preparing. The delightful scent of garlic and herbs was mouthwatering.

Bianca was really going to miss her.

"Oh!" the Panamanian woman yelped as she backed into me. "You startled me, Mrs.—"

"Please. Don't be so formal. It's just little old me."

"O-okay." She disapproved of how tight my clothes were. Of what I wore and how I wore it. I made her nervous. I knew that after today, she'd be stirring things up in this house. Maybe try to have Tanner kick me out.

I grabbed Lorenda and hugged her. "There. Isn't this better?"

"Ma'am?"

"Don't I feel good, Lorenda?" I stressed *good* the way Halle did in *Monster's Ball*.

"I . . . I don't know. I guess. I have to cook."

"Yes. You do," I said, whispering in her ear. "That roast smells delicious . . . almost heavenly. Mmmm. I can taste it already," I purred as if in the throes of pleasure. I held back a giggle as Lorenda's body quivered.

"Ma'am, please let me go."

"But I like hugging you." I began rubbing suggestively on her back. The woman's big breasts heaved into me in surprise. I could've sworn she was almost in tears.

"And . . . and I'd like you to stop. Please."

"You don't mean that."

"Yes, I do," she pleaded. "I have to get the roast out. It's done."

I cocked my head to the side, the better to look her eye-to-eye. "You like my sister better than me, huh?"

"I . . . I don't know what you're talking about. Now please let me go."

"You don't like the way I hold you?" I brushed my tongue against her ear.

"No." Her voice was barely audible. I think she was praying.

I slid my hands down to her ample ass. And squeezed hard. "Does this feel better?"

Lorenda yelped and bucked, knocking me back. She charged at me in tears, swinging wildly in an end-over-end flailing motion. It ended quickly as she ran past, howling for all to hear. I heard the door slam to the quarters she used when staying overnight.

"That was way too easy," I remarked smugly, left alone in the kitchen.

The scent got to me again. I closed my eyes, savoring it for a second. The oven mitts had been left out. I placed my hands in them and removed the roast from the oven.

Humming innocently, I helped myself to a large piece of roast, then sat down to enjoy. I was going to miss Lorenda's cooking. Thanksgiving was around the corner too. I hoped Bianca could cook, because I sure as hell couldn't.

The slice of roast went into my mouth, allowing me to savor the garlic and herbs.

Mmm, mmm, good.

14

HENRY

I rushed back to the Radisson, where I'd checked in. A few days ago, I had drunkenly considered robbing my former boss. Now I carried a backpack filled with more than I expected to get from him. God working in mysterious ways, as the old adage goes.

A deep calmness overtook me as I inserted my card key into the lock. That calmness was my undoing. As I swung my door open, I was rushed. A hard shoulder block and I went spilling along with the backpack onto my room floor.

Because of my cast, the backpack slipped off my arm. It tumbled clumsily along until it bumped into the coffee table. My instincts stopped me from scrambling for it.

Kash obviously felt like getting his cardio in. He kicked at me, but I blocked it with my cast. He thought about kicking again, but wasn't used to the physical stuff. He seemed to almost pout as he put his foot down. Lupe joined him in the room and had no such issues. With Kash's approval, he swung and hit, eliciting a groan from me.

"Whassup, Henry?" Kash said as he plopped onto the hotel couch. He had an apple in his hand that he was eyeing. "Did you know that you have better security at this hotel than at your expensive apartment? We had a hard time tracking you down in here. Were you trying to hide, Henry?"

Lupe stood near the backpack. His eyes began following mine, but I quickly looked away from it. "No. I just came here to hook up with someone."

Kash and Lupe exchanged glances. Both of them began grinning. "You're not buying hoes, is ya? Paying for that pussy?" Kash asked.

"No," I offered, afraid to get off the floor. Lupe liked to play that game: Make you think it was cool, then knock you the fuck back down.

"Okay. 'Cause I would be mad if you weren't going through me for those services. Seein' as we got a close relationship 'n' all. So, where she at?"

"She's coming. Later."

"I bet she will be 'coming,' " he joked. "That the same one you had on display in your window?"

I moved, almost rising to my feet. Lupe flinched and I stopped on the spot.

"Yeah. We watchin' you," Kash answered. "And *that* was a good show. Man, Windex ain't cleanin' that. Wish I had some binoculars. Think we should wait for your friend to come by? I'd like to see that shit up close."

"She's not down for that."

Kash eyed me. Nothing said. Just those cold eyes peering beyond the obvious. I wondered if he could smell the money beneath his nose. I felt a chill. I usually ended up visiting the ER when he got quiet. He sprang up, making me jerk. "Nah. We gonna give you some privacy. Would be a shame to let this fine room go to waste." He finally took a bite of his apple, spit flying as he chomped away.

He and Lupe turned to leave. I began to breathe, feeling in the clear and spared more pain. I glanced at the backpack again on reflex. Stupid. Lupe caught my eyes and decided to speak.

"What's in the bag?" he grunted.

"Clothes," I said in as calm a voice as I could muster. "She likes to role-play."

Lupe chuckled as he looked at his boss. "Toldja he was a freak."

I grinned, allowing them to dismiss me. I was closing the door when Kash held it up with his hand. His jovial demeanor had snapped back.

"Why ya ain't at work today, Henry?"

"Huh?" was all I could muster before Lupe blindsided me. I fell again, this time holding my nose.

Tears formed in my eyes as the two assumed the familiar stance over my battered body. "You can't keep secrets in this town. I know you lost your job. I can't trust you, Henry. And here I thought you were my boy," he spat with a grin of malice. "Now I want all my money by next week. Every last dime."

I groaned. "My car. You can have it." I began to offer whatever was in the backpack, but something held me back.

Kash rolled his eyes. "If I wanted a sports car, I'd own one. Don't play me. That shit's leased. Besides, that car makes it easy to find you in this town." As he rolled out for real this time, he left me with parting words: "Next week, Henry. Next week."

"Payday," Lupe taunted as he slammed the hotel door shut behind them.

I waited for my pulse to slow and the soreness in my nose to subside. Only when I was certain they wouldn't return did I crawl over to the backpack.

I plopped the orange carrier onto the small dining table and pulled up a chair. It was time to finally see what Pumpkin had delivered.

"Housekeeping," a woman yelled from the hallway right as I was unzipping.

"Go away!" I yelled back. Back to the matter at hand. I opened it like a candy bar.

The smell of crisp bills was intoxicating. Just how much was in here? I had thought about counting it earlier as I drove, but was afraid to wipe out, seeing as I had a cast on my hand. As I continued pulling out stack after stack, I was glad I'd waited.

When I was finished, I sat there in stunned silence. It took time to set in.

Eighty-five thousand dollars.

A woman I'd just met, and whom I barely knew, had dropped eighty-five K on me.

It was too quiet in here. I walked over to the remote, turning on the TV before returning to the counted loot.

"Wow." I gasped, realizing the options before me.

Would Kash take this and let me off the hook? Or would he take it, then break a few more pieces of me? I could use it to get out of town, maybe start over fresh. I wanted to call Pumpkin and get some more answers, but with the number blocked I'd have to wait.

"I really like the Cleveland/Atlanta game," the voice on the TV said as if talking to me. I turned around, seeing the men in suits analyzing this weekend's matchup. I gazed, mesmerized at the formulas and magic numbers understood by risk takers such as myself. My palms became sweaty. A lump formed in my throat. It was hard to look away, but I did.

And picked up the phone.

The wire felt firm when I stepped out onto it.

"Henry?" the man on the other end asked. I hadn't dealt with him in years.

"Yeah. It's me."

"Kash ain't done kilt you?"

I laughed, pretending to be confident. "Nah, man. Things are okay with Kash." If the cast on my hand had been a sock puppet, it would've been shaking its head to the contrary. "Check this out. I need to get in on a game this weekend. Big."

"Uh-huh." He sighed. "Look. Kash spread the word. Your credit ain't so hot right now. I mean . . . I'd love to help you, but . . ."

"I'm talking cash money."

"Oh." There was a long, drawn-out silence. Then he collected himself. "I'm listening," he said.

"Good."

My balance was sure as I took my first step. You just never looked below.

15

BIANCA

Chaos.

I awoke to chaos. It was Tanner in the distance who jarred me awake. His raised voice always carried so much bass. I was on my bed now, a pillow under my head and a throw draped over me. Doctor's orders were something to follow, as I was learning. Under my hand rested a tiny slip of paper.

Pumpkin.

Just a short note saying she was sorry for upsetting me and that she would explain later. Remembering my experience at the bank pissed me off again. I balled up the piece of paper and threw it on the side of the bed. She'd better have a damn good explanation.

Yawning, I shook off my cobwebs and went to check on the commotion. Downstairs Tanner was arguing with someone at our front door. I prayed he hadn't discovered Pumpkin was visiting.

But Lorenda had heard the two of us fighting.

"No, Mr. Coleman. I must go," Lorenda pleaded desperately. What was she saying? And why was she blubbering? I hurried down the stairs to investigate, fearful that it might be too late.

"Lorenda, what's wrong?" I asked as I ran up on them. Tanner looked obviously frustrated.

She saw me and spat out something in Spanish. She picked up her hastily stuffed bag from the floor and began heading out the door. It looked permanent. Tanner tried stopping her again.

"Move, Mr. Coleman. I can't stay here."

I began crying, feeling the one constant slipping away, never to return. I went to give her a hug, but she wasn't having it. "Get away. Don't touch me," she shrieked. "I must go. Now!"

"Lorenda, wait. Please. Is it something we've done? Is it something I've done? We can talk."

She glared at me in such a way that I was frightened.

"This . . . this is a crazy house," was her final condemnation as she fled for the elevator.

Tanner and I stood in the doorway, waiting for our now former housekeeper to catch the elevator. For a full minute we waited in the hope that she would return.

"Know anything about this?" he asked.

"No."

"Hmm. Well, there goes the best housekeeper I've ever had." He threw his arms up in frustration. He went back inside, urging me to follow and close the door.

"There goes the only housekeeper I've ever had," I mumbled, my heart feeling more than the relationship between employer and employee. You might say Lorenda had been the closest I'd had to a mother since . . .

"Bianca, close the door. She's gone."

"Okay."

"You can't let this get you down, Bianca." Tanner tasted his soup. He looked impeccable in his dark suit and crisp white shirt, having ordered for both of us earlier. He'd coaxed me to Figueroa, one of the finest establishments in town, thinking a night out would lift my spirits. With the events earlier, my appetite wasn't up to par. If he'd known everything, his wouldn't be either.

"I can't help it. This has been a day from hell. I'm sorry that I'm being a downer on our evening. I think I just need to go to bed."

The mention of bed in that context bothered him. I believe he was expecting a full-blown evening out tonight . . . with dessert later. "What did the doctor say?" he asked.

"I'm fine. Just stressed out."

He chuckled in the middle of a spoonful of bisque. "I really don't see what you have to be stressed out about."

"You have no idea," I muttered. I hated when he took that tone.

"Want to tell me?" His spoon clinked in the empty bowl as he wiped his mouth with the napkin. "Are your shoe shipments arriving too late for the spring collection or something? Is that your idea of stress? The mayor will be appointing me as chair on his inner-city development committee next week. I'm supposed to come up with a plan for Hunter's Green . . . without bulldozing the hellhole. Now, *that's* stress."

My cell rang in my purse, stopping me from being less prudent with my comeback. I decided to answer it and use that time to cool down.

"Hey, girl," Rory said. "Sorry I missed your call earlier. Issues with Morris's father. Your message said you were at the doctor. Everything okay?"

"Yeah. It was nothing. Thanks for calling me. Look, I'm going to call you tomorrow. I'm at dinner right now."

"Out? Like in a restaurant?"

"Yes. Me and Tanner."

"About time Mr. Clucker got with the program. Wine and dine and maybe a sixty-nine. Something I swear by."

I laughed. "Good night. I'll talk to you later." As I hung up, I accidentally hit the wrong button. It showed recent calls, many I didn't recognize. They'd been blocked with a *67 too, so my number wouldn't be identified. I dropped my cell back in my purse, too weary to worry about it now.

"Rory?" Tanner asked, already knowing the answer. I smiled and nodded. "At least the whore gives you a lift."

"Tanner, I've told you how I feel about the name-calling. And just what's that supposed to mean, anyway?"

"Nothing. I'm just ticked that she can bring the most energy out of you that I've seen in days. Just thought we could go out after this . . . see the sights. But sleep is all that's on your mind."

I sighed. He didn't mean the riverfront or Cray Gardens. Visits to the spot he had in mind always left me feeling dirty. "How about next week?" I feebly offered.

"Can't. I'll be busy with the committee you just ignored. Remember?"

"I guess I'll have to make it up to you." I did my best to project enthusiasm, although I was never good at faking it. In order to fully please him, I almost had to become another person.

"Uh-huh," he grunted as he looked at our entrées being brought over.

Although the rest of our meal was delicious, the conversation was limited. *Stunted*, perhaps, was a better word.

At least I'd be taking my sleep aid on a full stomach.

16

PUMPKIN

"**I**'m here," I spoke into the receiver.

As I exited the cab at the Radisson, I admired the new Motorola cell phone I'd purchased. The custom color matched my eyes perfectly. Bianca's old Nokia lacked a sense of style, just like her. At least with the money I now had, I would no longer have to use hers.

After tipping the cabdriver, I tightened the trench coat I was wearing.

Cold night tonight.

And I'm the coldest, I whimsically thought from behind my designer shades as my stilettos one-two-stepped into the lobby.

The atrium was bisected by trails of guests returning from their evenings. It was that time for most. Drunken conventioneers, shuffling back to their beds with incredible tales of things terribly un-incredible. I stood in their midst, a rock dropped in the middle of swarming ants, parting the wave as I looked and waited.

Two characters looked out of place in the lobby—more Holiday Inn or Motel 6 types, if you asked me. The big black one looked like he had asthma . . . I could imagine an inhaler strapped inside his black leather jacket where a gun would probably go. The pale one looked to be Spanish or something, with a dash of *el negro* thrown in. Even though they huddled close, looking shifty, I didn't figure them to be gay. They were waiting for someone too.

It had better not be Henry, I thought. I started to call him, tell him I'd meet him in back or something.

But he was already emerging from the hallway elevator. A dark Italian suit was his choice for the night . . . my suggestion. He probably had to sneak back to his place to get it. I liked the cuff links he'd picked too. The man could be impressive if not for his shortcomings. Probably needed a good woman for guidance. He was a fun pastime and eager to please. Unfortunately he was a broke *and* broken man, and Pumpkin wasn't one for reconstruction projects.

I buried the thought to motion to him. He'd already seen me, but I wanted him aware of the two men now standing. It was too late, so I decided to get to him first.

Grabbing his arm, I placed a kiss on him before he could inquire about my unusual appearance for our evening out.

"To your left," I hissed for only him to hear. I felt

the flinch go through his body, revealing who the architects of his pain were.

I tried to push him in the opposite direction, but his resolve seemed to strengthen.

"It's all right," he said calmly. "Just some friends of mine."

I stayed in his arms, turning to face the ogres. We were in a hotel lobby, but you never knew what people were capable of. I was living testament to that.

"We're going to be late," I reminded him.

"Shit, Henry. That's her, ain't it?" The dark one's mouth creased. Looked like he wanted to taste me. "Your window washer? Lupe, she's . . ."

"Amazing," Lupe finished. Yeah. I got that a lot. And that was before they felt the flow.

"Henry, shouldn't you be out working on my money?"

"And shouldn't you be out working on a diet?" I snapped. Sorry. Couldn't help it. His ass had it coming. Henry's grasp on me tightened.

"Bitch got a smart mouth, Henry." *No, he did not just ignore me.* "Would love to put it to work."

"You don't know who you're messing with, you fuckin' frog," I spat. "I will—"

Henry cut me off. "Kash, c'mon, man. I'm trying to have a nice evening with my woman. We can deal with this later."

"Sure will, boy. And it ain't gonna be fingers." Lupe made a cracking sound.

"I gotcha, Kash. Don't worry. You're my boy. And I gotcha." He patted Kash on his shoulder in an unusually calm, upbeat manner. He then led me away.

"Time is ticking, Henry."

"I know. I know," he answered, not bothering to look back.

As we sped away in his car, I had to know.

"What did you do with the money I gave you? I mean . . . you paid them, right?"

"Pumpkin, I don't know where we're going, but you are on fire." He laughed like a madman.

"They wouldn't have been there if you'd paid them. What the fuck did you do, Henry?" I groaned, briefly removing my shades.

"Relax. I did the smart thing. That would've only been an extension." He slowed for construction on the turnpike. Once past, he accelerated again and continued with his train of thought. "Made an investment."

I didn't like it, didn't like it at all. Men like that didn't give many second chances. It looked to me like Henry was on his third.

He followed my instructions, arriving at the docks. I could sense his nervousness about the surroundings, the same as the night we'd met. Cute. A couple of turns on the uneven dark streets and we'd found a valet parking lot. It was unusual for the area and for the time of night, but he listened to me when I said it would be okay. After surrendering his keys to the fine sports car, we left down the adjacent alley on our journey.

"Kinda late for dinner?" he asked, probing in his own nervous yet cute way.

"Keep walking," I said.

He stared, expecting something to jump from the shadows and crawl spaces all around us. A rat scurried by, on the hunt for a late-night snack. I heard Henry's breathing change at the sight, but didn't break my pace. Half a block farther, I suddenly stopped. My partner for the night, still looking around, ran into me. He wasn't given a chance to apologize.

An imposing figure emerged from an unmarked door, amused at Henry's routine.

I approached him.

"Invitation only, ma'am," he said.

I lowered my shades, expecting the challenge. "You mean I came dressed up for nothing?" I undid the trench, revealing the French maid outfit to both him and Henry. "I thought I had an open invitation, seeing as I turned this place out last time I dropped by."

When he was finished eyeing the merchandise I had on display, he smiled. His eyes came back to mine.

"Yeah. You've been here before." He chuckled. "And with that kind of attitude, you can't help but be welcome." He stood aside, turning the knob and pulling the heavy old door ajar. Sounds greeted us from deep within, calling out to me. My heart began pumping, giving up its refrain. Leaving my trench undone, I entered. The doorman had let me past, but decided to press Henry some more . . . see if he really knew where he was, or if he really belonged. The suit certainly helped, but his jitters were a detriment. I could hear the questions playing in my companion's head.

"He's okay. He's my prop for the night." Shaking his head, the doorman granted Henry safe passage after checking his cast for anything that could be concealed.

Immediately upon entering, we descended the stairwell into the basement below.

"Is this a club?"

"Of a sort," I said. Low, measured tones best for the evening.

"I've never heard of this place. And I've been everywhere in this town."

"Grow up, junior. That's because this place doesn't exist. It's a dream you never forget."

Reaching the main floor, we were treated to the hedonistic thumpings of the Pussycat Dolls' "Loosen Up My Buttons." Dark purple velvet adorned the walls, with black leather furniture as accents. Another imposing figure with a walkie-talkie took my trench, bestowing upon me a stylized face mask to

wear. Henry followed suit, looking at the other patrons before donning his. Couples shuffled by in the
wide hallway, faces obscured like ours by the beautiful custom creations. At the hall's end, you could
see it opened to a larger space.

"How do you know of this place?" This Twenty
Questions of his was becoming trying.

I paused, allowing another beat to flow over me
before answering. I turned to him and draped my
arms around his neck. "Let's just say I got my start
here. Does that bother you?"

I waited for a response. After longer than I expected, it finally came. "No."

"Good. Remember that dream I just mentioned?"

"Yeah."

"It's a wet one," I teased.

Before he could say anything, I kissed Henry, allowing our tongues to mingle. I stopped abruptly,
leaving him wanting as I escorted him by his tie like
a slave toward what awaited us.

17

HENRY

I think she was just tiring of my questions.

"It's a rule here," she whispered from beneath her decorative cover. The puffy white headdress rested atop her short, curly wig, obscuring her features some more. "No talking, unless . . ."

"Unless what?"

With a smile, she looked at me. "You'll figure it out."

I think I was.

From beneath the mask that made my nose itch, I watched. People of all colors—some in costumes, some in formal wear—politely interacted. Some danced. Some pranced. Others mingled. Various smaller rooms branched off from the large open area where we stood. Other couples, sometimes in groups of three or four, discreetly entered them as we stood by. Some weren't bothering with a semblance of privacy. I began to understand the language. Why bother speaking when just a wink or the tilt of a head would suffice . . . or accomplish so much more? I watched a pairing in the shadows—a tall, slender vision of chocolate loveliness and her long-haired boy toy—with intense curiosity. She was clad in nothing but a teddy and matching heels, gladly accepting the passionate assault of his lips as they trickled along the expanse of her neck. The slow, rhythmic motion of their bodies as he stood behind her revealed there was more than kissing taking place.

Her legs buckled as she thrust herself against him, his defined arms firmly secured to her tapered waist. Their bodies clapped together, his open slacks falling to his knees. I felt uncomfortable watching, but didn't look away as they continued. I couldn't. Other guests gathered in a rough circle, feeling the same stirrings I was experiencing.

Then the woman in the center of the sexual circuit spoke—heavenly callings from someone in her own private nirvana at the moment.

"Oh! Oh! Yessss. Don't stop."

No talking, unless . . .

I now stood enlightened.

I shared a glance with my maid *de soir*. We nodded simultaneously. Time to move on. She took me by the hand to show me more.

The people in this dark, secret place had a familiarity to them. Before being fired, I had probably interacted with some. Their demeanor revealed them to be rich and powerful. If they weren't, then they certainly were beautiful. Both groups came with certain advantages. The no-talking rule allowed the whole lot to avoid being identified in the less freaky world above.

None held my fascination as much as Pumpkin. I wondered how she came to get her start in such a place. As we interacted with other couples, she wore their lustful looks and playful touches, both male and female alike, like a badge of honor. I was so engrossed in my surroundings that I'd missed the feather duster at her side, which she was playfully swishing at people. Her maid skirt swung on cue with every spin. The outfit was ironic in that she chose to be the servant tonight when reality proclaimed her to be the master.

I just followed faithfully, accepting the surreal as a masked woman or two gave a passing grope or kiss my way. Tomorrow, my luck would be changing. Being with Pumpkin tonight was just another affirmation.

A nude woman, painted brightly like a tiger, made her way to us, offering tablets that were probably Viagra. On a cart behind her were various drinks. A man near us stopped her, helping himself to a glass of what looked to be brandy and one of the blue pills. His suit was similar to mine, making both of us smile in admiration. His companion for the night was a nice-looking blond woman in a fitted black evening gown. Couldn't give her perfect marks because her face was obscured. An unusual tattoo of an apple within a heart was displayed on her shoulder. The brother appeared older . . . distinguished, so I'm sure she was a dime—*paid for on his dime*. I smirked over the mental pun as I took a glass of wine from the tigress. No Viagra for me. I was just here to watch, anyway. I think.

Pumpkin saw me observing our friends, as she was herself. The four of us smiled cordially with that "what are we gonna do now?" vibe filling the air. Pumpkin ended it with a motion of her head to follow.

And we did.

I glimpsed inside one of the occupied rooms as we passed. In there I blinked, unable to count the mass of tangled bodies engaging in multiple sexual acts. One woman hung upside down over the side of the massive bed in there, her face in ecstasy as she received from the man above her. I watched her teeth clench, then suddenly release as she gasped under the ferocity of his strokes. When I looked back, Pumpkin and our two friends had entered the next room. I stole a fleeting glance, then quickly joined them.

Maybe I was interested in more than observing.

We sat mesmerized. Me? My pants were about to burst.

The other man and I removed our jackets, sitting in leather chairs at opposite corners of the tiny room. Pumpkin and the woman in the gown had undressed each other for our pleasure, kissing and sucking along the way. Somehow they kept the masks on, proceeding to lie across the bed as they took turns eating each other's pussy. When it was Pumpkin's turn, she turned her ass to me, winding it around hypnotically as she buried her head between the blonde's legs. Maybe it was just the day's events overcoming me or the good wine in my glass. The warm spot between her legs seemed to be an eye, taunting me . . . daring me to take a stab as its familiar sweetness reached my nose. In my pants, I rose at its command.

"Oh, shit! Oh, shit!" Blondie whooped as her spiked heels popped up in the air as if on springs. Pumpkin didn't seem to mind the commotion she was causing; her tongue dialed in on every button the woman had. Push. Push. Push.

The other man had finished his glass of brandy, gulping it down. He rose, quickly unbuttoning his shirt. Viagra had claimed him. Wood for days, putting me to shame. As he'd been here before, I followed his lead. Even with my cast, I beat him undressing. *Take that, Viagra.*

The women saw us approach the bed, but Pumpkin's victim seemed rather caught up in the moment. When my girl stopped the pleasuring, I sensed regret. I guess no one knows a woman like another woman. Blondie moved on, though. The man had just climbed onto the bed when she motioned him closer. I watched her lips form a seal as she took his dick in her mouth. She hummed as she slurped and sucked . . . almost to the beat.

The other woman fresh on her lips, Pumpkin pulled me atop her, where she shared a taste. As we kissed harder and harder, I had to have her. Pumpkin was my drug, drawing me in on so many levels. The physical claimed me now, demanding my full, undivided attention. I gently slid inside, ready to fuck her like she'd never been fucked.

As we continued our adventure, our friends had moved on. Having had his dick and balls sucked on, he put her on hands and knees and entered from the back. Her ass jiggled as he proceeded to fuck her doggy style. She shuddered with every thrust, apparently trying to remember to breathe.

A twisted contest developed between me and the man I hardly knew. In business and pleasure, some rules were the same. The harder he went, the harder I went, sweat forming on my chest as wetness flowed onto the bed. Pumpkin and his friend's rising moans of delight and curses of pleasure were our guides, each of us wanting to declare mastery of our partner.

Looking up at me, Pumpkin smiled as tears welled up in her eyes. I was pleased to please her as she had done for me. She began to laugh unexpectedly, exploding with a gush of nectar onto my probing dick. The woman's face came closer, thrust across the bed by her unrelenting partner.

Pumpkin hadn't noticed until her flailing arm bumped the woman's mask.

It popped free, tumbling onto the bed beside them.

All ceased.

"Excuse me," Pumpkin apologized, opening her eyes to fix on the exposed face.

"It's okay," the woman answered, neither one obeying the rules now. The woman, a beautiful face on her, paused. "Do I know you?" she asked as she reached for her ornate disguise.

Still inside her, I felt Pumpkin's muscles tense. Not from an orgasm. "None of us knows anyone in here," she replied with a smile different from the message her body was conveying to me.

Before the woman could comment further, Pumpkin had motioned for me to get up. I complied, but with a bit of disappointment. We gathered our stuff and hurriedly left our friends on the bed and thoroughly confused. She barely got her mask back in place before the man began fucking her again. And we were an afterthought. Viagra is a drug of neither patience nor understanding.

.   .   .

"What happened back there?" I asked. I drove with the windows lowered lest my car be consumed by the evidence of our consummation. I also needed the night air to cool me down and allow me to think.

"Nothing," she offered. "I just remembered I needed to get back."

"To your sister's? Aren't you too old for a curfew?"

"We never outgrow rules of some sort." I didn't think she was in the car with me at the moment.

I remembered the directions without her saying, almost repeating the course I'd taken during our first encounter. She seemed more fragile now . . . or maybe it was anger. Too much silence to determine; I drove on.

She'd left her trench coat at the club. Outside the apartment, I offered my jacket, but she wouldn't have it. Just ran inside, sticking a hand up to stop the doorman from any inquiries.

One day I would have to camp out here. Find out more about this Pumpkin. Looking at my watch, I knew it would wait for some other time. After midnight, it was now game day. The day all my luck would change in dramatic fashion.

Maybe I would tell Kash to go fuck himself once I gave him his money.

Looking at my cast resting on the steering wheel, I left that decision for later.

In drive, I sped away into the late night.

18

BIANCA

"Go to bed," Dad tells me.

Company's over. I don't want to go to bed. Why do I always have to go to bed?

He tucks me in, but can't make me stay. I close my eyes and count until I think he's gone. When I run out of numbers, I sit up in my bed. I hug my Molly Wonder doll, knowing he will be mad.

Me and Molly Wonder sneak out of my room. Maybe company's gone and I can sleep with him and Mom. Molly Wonder would like that.

It's all dark. I don't like the dark except when I'm asleep.

Mom and Dad's room is at the far end of the hallway. I can see a light under their door.

Good.

Dad's visitor is gone. And Mom and Dad are still awake.

Me and Molly Wonder move faster, feeling our way down the long, dark hallway. I hear talking and tell Molly

Wonder to be quiet. She listens. She always does. That's why she's my best friend.

The knob turns before I get there. Their bedroom door opens.

"Daddy!" I gasp. He hasn't heard me. Doesn't see me and Molly Wonder yet.

He stands in the doorway to their bedroom. He's wearing his white shorts, like after he gets out of the shower. I think he's smoking a cigarette. Those stink.

The door opens further.

I bolted awake. Why was my heart racing? I had the feeling that I was in a strange place, but it was my bedroom. Tanner nuzzled up next to me, reaffirming things as he snored. I couldn't sleep any more. Not the way I felt. I gently lifted his arm and slid out.

I ran a bubble bath instead of my usual shower. It seemed to work on the aches I was feeling. Probably a restless night of sleep, or Tanner crowding my side of the bed. Soaking, I read a few pages from the novel *Satin Nights*, the sequel to Karen E. Quinones Miller's *Satin Doll* that I had been anticipating for years. It was like visiting with old friends, something I wished I had had more of while growing up.

Before turning into a prune, I exited the tub. With Lorenda gone, I would be foraging for breakfast this morning. In our bedroom, Tanner surprised me by being awake. He'd already put on a pair of shorts and was tying the laces on his running shoes.

"Not sleeping late? I missed your coming in last

night." No shock, as I'd taken a sleep aid, per doctor's orders.

"I wasn't gone long," Tanner replied, looking vibrant as ever. "Tomorrow's the usual grind so I need to get my cardio in now. How do you feel?"

"Better. Thank you. Would you like me to fix you some breakfast?"

"Maybe when I return," he answered with a kiss to my cheek. "I'm going to hit some laps at Crestwood Park. That track they laid helps with my knees." He was such a healthy person that I forgot the occasional weaknesses brought on by his age and hectic schedule.

With some quiet time alone, I decided to paint my toenails before burning toast for myself. Pumpkin burst through the bedroom doorway, making me spill polish on the carpet.

"Shit, Pumpkin!" I yelled.

"That's the spirit," she joked, not caring about the mess she was responsible for. She skipped right over my hand as I tried to dab at the red stain with a piece of tissue.

"When are you leaving? You're causing way too much trouble for me."

She helped herself to a seat in the wingback chair by the window. She wore gray sweat bottoms and a white sports bra. She let one leg dangle over the arm as the sun glinted in her eyes. "Ooooh, I'm not sure, sis. I'm having the time of my life. Especially last night." She cackled, full of mischief. "Nothing like a good sex party to get me going. All that fucking and sucking."

"Y'know . . . you don't have to talk like that. And next time, spare me the details of your troubled life."

"Shit. My life ain't the one that's troubled."

Our eyes locked, making me remember our tussle in this very room. The doctor had told me to take it easy. No stress. I calmed myself, then spoke. "I want my money back, sis."

She popped out of the wingback like a jackrabbit, suddenly antsy. She flicked her hair defiantly with her fingers as she viewed herself in my mirror. "Can't do that. It's been invested. At least, that's what he tells me."

"He? Who are you talking about, Pumpkin?"

"None of your concern. Why don't you go fix breakfast for your husband? He'll be back from his jog soon."

"You were spying?"

"Nah. The two of you talking woke me up. Heaven knows, I need some beauty sleep after all that . . . activity." The faces and gestures she made were obscene. "Anyway, I guess I'll see you later."

"Where are you going?"

"Out. Get some air. Maybe do a little jogging myself. Staying this fine takes work, babe. You want to come?"

I took another fruitless dab at the drying polish. "No. I'll stay here."

She came over and leaned in front of me. "Why? Afraid of what you might find?" she asked wickedly. I just stared, taking pity. She ran her fingers through my short curls before planting a disturbing kiss on my forehead and jogging out of the room. She actually whistled.

19

PUMPKIN

What a lovely day to be in the park.

I knew it was that bastard Tanner at the sex club. No frilly mask could hide that ego nor hide the motions of his body, of which I was aware. And now I knew the woman who was his companion for the night. All it took was an *accidental* unveiling to be sure.

Surprise, surprise.

He thought he had games on Bianca. Of course, he had yet to learn that I was the master of games.

Standing on the trail, sheltered by the large oak's limbs, I saw people impatiently jog around me. I wasn't here for that. Their scowls and beleaguered mutterings simply rolled off. Teflon sweats with a matching bra and panties.

I spied the mighty Mr. Coleman going through the motions, but not really into it like these other sweaty fools. A woman with a baby stroller was on the trail ahead of him, kneeling as she tended to her child. Shades similar to mine obscured her eyes. The masks we wore every day. Their illusion was only temporary. Nothing could hide us from who we truly were.

When he reached the pair, he slowed to a walk. Then he stopped, taking several quick glances at his surroundings before breaking into conversation with her. She looked up from her child and smiled, enamored with his attention.

Rather than stir up the Kool-Aid, I decided to watch some more, let the sugar settle on the bottom. A pretzel stand was nearby, so I ordered a big one and waited for things to go down. I found a bench and took a seat to feast on my snack. Unhealthy for this time of day, but I didn't care.

The woman stood up again, continuing her exchange with Tanner. Both of them were smiling over something undoubtedly terribly lame.

My view was cut off. I licked the salty butter off my fingers and stretched my neck around the temporary obstruction—a man and his dog. He still wasn't moving. Appropriate for where I was at, I guess.

"Don't I know you?"

Damn. He wasn't leaving, was he? A suck of my fingertip and I decided to acknowledge him. "I think not," I offered. *Move, man!*

Man had a gleeful lilt in his tone. "Are you sure?" he pressed. His cute little Yorkie sniffed the ground. I gave him another look. Only because he had a cute dog.

Oh, I mentally registered.

Way too small a world.

The man was Henry's looky-looky neighbor whom I'd provided a window view of my goods. The scholarly one was out for a stroll, but the peep show was closed.

"Yes. I think I do remember you now."

"Really?" he gushed. The man was about to drop his dog's leash and do the Cabbage Patch.

"Sure. Aren't you from the clinic?"

"The clinic?" He decided not to drop that leash too quickly.

"Yes. I work where we perform surgeries. Didn't you come in Tuesday for the 'change' consultation?" I gave him a hot wink.

Red was the color of his face. *Very* red.

"You must have me mistaken," he blubbered. He resumed his walk, the four-legged mustache being yanked along.

See man run.

Tanner and the two had moved off the trail. A nearby tree provided them some cover, but I still had the perfect view.

For someone cold, smug, and aloof, Tanner was displaying way too much joy as he removed the small child from its stroller. Cute little boy, from what I could see. His mother placed her hand on

Tanner's back and rubbed approvingly. As he held the baby up to the sky, cooing like a fool, I recognized that look.

All masks eventually got lifted.

Hmph. No more pretzel.

I wiped my hands and disappeared before I was noticed.

Not the time. Not the time.

20

HENRY

Sunday at a sports bar. A normal occurrence for me in recent years, except for a different location this time—next door to the Radisson where I foolishly thought I could hide. Here I was seeking the familiar—the series of highs and lows I so desperately craved.

A craving was a want . . . a desire. A need was a necessity.

I had a need to win today.

I guess you could say my life depended on it.

I felt good.

I was a winner. In spite of all the turmoil, in spite of my horrible luck, I was still standing. I was a winner.

Another round of drinks for the place. Another wave of cheers in my honor. I was very popular at the moment. Just like Cleveland was on the scoreboard.

I had the lead I needed. The cash money I'd delivered earlier in the day was already multiplying. Like those gremlins from that old movie, fresh off a splash of water.

"If you keep buying me drinks, you're going to get me drunk," the woman seated to my left at the bar teased, detecting my swagger. She slid the fresh glass of wine over and tasted from it. Lips lingering on the glass long enough for me to notice. The unspoken equated to: *Wouldn't you like to know what happens when I get drunk?* Before meeting Pumpkin, I would've been finding out in quick order. That was just it. She wasn't Pumpkin. Couldn't hold that thong on her best day, but I continued to let her think she had a spot on my roster. Options. Definitely feeling like old times.

Some wore their allegiances in the open—team colors. Others stood, revealed by their outbursts to the referees' calls. I was more discreet . . . especially with the underdog, Cleveland, leading through most of the game. No need to be emotional. Quiet confidence was what I exuded. To most, you'd think I didn't have a vested interest in the game.

To most.

There were others in here sharing the same compulsion. That taste you get in the back of your mouth, that quickening of the pulse at the change of a score or end of a game. No matter how differently we dressed or how different our social statuses, we knew one another. We were brothers in the grip.

Yes. Enough wires in here for a fucking acrobat convention.

"Who's playing?"

"Huh? Oh. Atlanta and Cleveland, I think," I answered nonchalantly. I was just here for camaraderie and idle chatter, maybe to take a fine thing like her back to my bed. I blinked right after the mental fibs.

Atlanta finally scored. A group of three men in their Atlanta jerseys paused from eating potato skins to pump their fists. Small glimmer of hope for them. Maybe what they would call a moral victory. Pity. Atlanta had been favored. And time was on my side.

"I don't know much about football," she admitted. But she did know something about cleavage. I checked the time remaining in the game and decided to give her a few more minutes of mine.

"What are you a fan of?" I turned completely toward her for the first time tonight.

"Hockey," she replied. "I like the way they work their sticks."

"Fan of the stick work?"

"Mmm-hmm." She grinned. An innocent giggle escaped a not-so-innocent mouth. My money was growing, and so was my hunger for her. Henry was back. I was so glad I hadn't put that bullet in my head.

"Are you a ballplayer?"

"No," I answered, certain my physique gave that away. It was a nice suit that I wore. Maybe she thought it concealed muscles. Or maybe my being a black man was her only reference. I then realized she was looking at my cast. "Accident at work."

"Poor baby."

The way she said it reminded me of Pumpkin. *Damn.* I wished she'd been around tonight to celebrate, especially since she'd made this all possible. But I didn't have her phone number. She'd be calling me. And I'd thank her.

The game was almost over. Cleveland was taking time off the clock. Up by three points in which they were favored to lose by the same amount. *And about to score again on Atlanta*, I smugly conceded. Kash would finally be off my back.

"We've been talking and you've never told me your name." I hinted at more beyond the bar. After the game.

She smiled, getting it.

The final drive to wrap it up was coming. Some of the watchers moved to the bar to better see the inevitable. Cleveland had time enough for a field goal, but was going for another touchdown. As the group in Atlanta jerseys began screaming, "Defense," Cleveland hiked the ball. And I smiled.

We all watched the quarterback as he scrambled away from the opposing team's defenders, large snarling cats wanting to plant him in the ground. And there it was.

A single Cleveland player, San Antonio Jackson,

running loose at the back of the end zone, waved frantically. I waited for that magic pass to end the game. I watched the quarterback spot him and cock back to throw.

I closed my eyes, envisioning the ball leaving his hand on its way to its destiny.

I was smiling when the hit came.

Neither I nor the quarterback saw Atlanta's linebacker streaking from his blind side, where he proceeded to do just that—blindside.

About half the place, including the Atlanta fans whose drinks I'd just paid for, erupted in cheers. Not for me this time. I wasn't being honored— Atlanta was.

Then the impossible.

The football's destiny wouldn't be in the hands of San Antonio Jackson, spinning at the feet of his latest celebration. It lay on the greenery of the field, rolling around as big as day.

No one from Cleveland noticed it. They were more concerned about their quarterback. *Fuck him. Get the ball. This game is over!* I begged mentally.

Someone heard my pleas. A pair of hands snatched the ball up, sensing what was afoot. And began running in the opposite direction.

Atlanta had the ball.

Their cornerback, Willis Wallace, was now darting down the field toward Atlanta's goal line as a wave of nausea overcame me.

The numbers on the field came and went, the announcer screaming them out with a glut of emotion.

"Wallace has the ball! Wallace has the ball! And he's off to the races!"

Somebody tackle his ass. Please.

"He's at the fifty, forty-five, forty, thirty-five, the thirty!"

Pain.

"The *twenty*!"

Agony.

"*Ten!*"

Disbelief.

"He could. Go. All. The waaaaaaaaay! Touchdown!"

No. Meltdown.

My cast began shaking. I grabbed it with my other hand, but it wouldn't stop.

The girl at the bar chose to answer me then. "My name can be whatever you like for the evening. Do you have a room here?" she whispered in my ear. Great. I was sitting with a call girl.

Worse.

I was in the hole just as when I came in. I'm sure Kash knew about the bet. Broke didn't matter when death might be imminent.

Broke.

Broken.

Both accurate descriptions regarding my present and future state. And why wouldn't my hand stop trembling?

"Are you okay? You look sick."

"Leave me alone."

"Excuse me?"

"Go away!" I shouted amidst the celebration. I stood up from the bar, grabbed my cast more firmly. I felt a vibration in my pocket as my cell phone rang. I checked the number. And felt like throwing up.

The wire I had just been bouncing precariously upon had snapped. I was still falling, but the pain I'd feel upon impact would be immeasurable.

Kash probably knew where I was.

I ran out of the sports bar, desperate and in a panic.

Eighty-five thousand dollars had been dropped in my lap and I blew it all to hell.

A man in free fall.

A few days ago, I hadn't thought it could get any worse.

21

BIANCA

We picked up the pace at the instructor's urging on this unusually mild Monday. There were several laps to go before we were finished. At my side was Rory, ever coordinated in her Nike attire. A good sweat was being generated in spinning class at the Brisbane Athletic Club. Part of our normal morning workout, stationary bikes strumming in harmony, as I tried to get back on course for the workweek and what lay ahead.

Wednesday, Tanner was to receive his appointment from the mayor. All the news channels would be covering such a grand occasion. Even though my role as the supportive wife was only to smile and look pretty for the cameras, it was taxing.

"Glad you could come this morning," Rory said in between her controlled breaths. "Thought I was going to have to get another partner."

"A girl misses a couple of days and you want to just trade her in? That sucks."

"Uh-huh." She chuckled. "Upgrade. I'd pick Weinstein over there, but she's too hot. Plastic surgeon for a husband." She added after a deep breath, "Probably too judgmental. She tried to crack about my wearing jewelry in class once. Once."

"So you're just keeping the ugly duckling around to make you look good?" I teased, mustering as homely a face as possible.

"Exactly. You're not just ugly; you're smart," she answered facetiously.

I threw my towel at her. She took it and dabbed the perspiration off her chest, then threw it back. The towel would be flung several more times as we rode out the remainder of the class.

After showering, we returned to the locker room to prepare for our respective days. Hers probably consisted of shopping for sales at Avery Mall, while mine consisted of ordering inventory from the wholesaler in New York. Work would be a break for me after all the mess going on at home. I was seriously debating telling Tanner about Pumpkin's arrival. As much as I feared the disasters that she brought on, I feared his reaction even more. But he had to maintain his focus. *Maybe after Wednesday*, I contemplated.

Rory seemed unusually chipper as she fastened the clasp on her sandals. She hummed some tune identifiable only by her. I was putting on my olive business suit, but slowed to observe. I speculated what it would be like to trade lives for a day.

"What?" she asked, bristling at the eyeballs she felt. "Do I have something in my hair?"

Of course not. It was flawless. "No. Just thinking about stuff."

She went back to fastening before her interest in my thoughts overrode it. "Anything you want to tell me? Because you can, y'know."

I considered unloading. About Lorenda leaving us, about Pumpkin's drama, and about how maybe, just maybe, Tanner's demands were beginning to wear me down.

"No," I politely replied instead. "Just day-dreaming."

Most of the other women had left. The remainder were either in the shower or in the process of exiting. Still, she whispered, "You're not cheating on Tanner, are you?"

I laughed. "Of course not. In spite of what he does, I don't roll like that. And the question's not what's so funny."

"Then what is?"

I regained my composure, deciding to share the private joke. "You didn't call him 'Mr. Clucker' this time."

"I didn't?" she muttered, stunned. She placed her sandal on the floor after finishing her task. She stood up, straightening her clothes and making sure her blond tresses were in place. "Oh, I don't call him that every time anyway."

"Whatever. Maybe you're becoming fond of him in your old age."

"Old? That's not ever happening. I'd be up in Weinstein's husband's office like that. And I'm not fond of Mr. Clucker. But back to my question . . . Are you out tippin'? Seriously. Maybe the doorman? Or the guy who makes your espresso, ooooh, so right?"

"I already said no, but why would you even ask that?"

She shrugged. "Something's different about you. Just seems like you've got secrets."

"No secrets. My life's too boring for secrets."

"So you do admit your life is lacking."

"What's going on? Are you suddenly a therapist? Those morning TV shows must be getting the best of you. Maybe you do need a job."

"Okay, okay. Now you're making me ill." She stuck her fingers in her mouth in a mock gagging motion.

We left the locker room together, but I had to stop after a few steps, my stomach suddenly upset.

Rory hadn't noticed me until she'd traveled a few feet, her gym bag dangling off her sculpted arm. "Something wrong?" she asked as she turned to look back.

"Uh . . . restroom. Might be a while," I sheepishly admitted. "Go on without me."

"Yeah. You don't want to be like that big girl

on *Flavor of Love.* No *deposits* in this place, please," she teased, commenting on the girl Flavor Flav had named "Somethin'." The programs that Rory watched religiously had ceased surprising me.

We said our good-byes; then I made a dash toward the ladies' room. The doctor had told me I wasn't pregnant, but I couldn't help but wonder what was wrong with me as I ran into an available stall.

22

PUMPKIN

I waited patiently, biding my time until Bianca cleared out. Little Miss Prissy was all alone as she exited the gym. It was a mild winter, but not *that* mild. She was reminded as a stiff wind blew across the parking lot. I watched her bristle, imagining goose bumps popping up on those fake-tanned arms of hers. I was too far away to see for sure. All I could make out was the tattoo. The one I'd seen before. That night at the sex club.

An apple inside a heart. On her shoulder.

An apple for Washington State.

Bianca said that bitch was from Seattle too. And here in the daylight, I found that she did remind me of someone. From long ago.

She triggered the remote on her burgundy Range Rover. I strode quickly, reaching into my pocket. I wasn't going to be fast enough.

She threw the bag in back, then entered the driver's seat. She slammed her door shut as I broke out into a run.

She put the Rover in reverse, its white taillights coming on. She'd barely moved before I tapped on the window. I slowed my breathing as I tried to look calm.

Confused at first, she mouthed something through the glass. Realizing I couldn't hear her, she lowered it.

She cracked a smile, feeling goofy over the window incident. She spoke. Said something warm and friendly. Familiar.

I didn't hear her.

Just made sure she was looking in my eyes.

No mask.

She said something else, no doubt wondering what I had to say or why I wasn't talking.

Then she looked harder, recognized the windows to my soul from that fateful night. Trick seemed confused.

My turn to smile.

"You shouldn't have messed with Tanner," I chided.

Sensing the wrong turn things had taken, she tried to respond . . . explain.

Tried.

Hard to speak when acid is being doused in your face . . . the eyes in particular. Yeah. Lorenda left some good cleaning supplies behind when I ran her off. A little mix of this and that and it was sure to do the job.

Bianca was being played by this bitch. Somebody had to have her back.

I walked off whistling, leaving Rory screaming in agony as she grasped at her face, her world permanently dark.

23

HENRY

'd checked out of my hotel as soon as I blew the game last night. One final charge on my credit card. The last twelve hours of ducking and dodging had me spent.

I had no appetite, but needed to keep up my energy. I quickly chewed the sausage croissant, rubbery as it was, and swallowed. Lurking in a parking lot behind Burger King was not a top choice for someone accustomed to dining at places lacking a ninety-nine-cent menu. *Either formulate a plan or fight,* I deluded myself. I was worthless in a fight and knew it. My desperation was tearing me apart, weakening my rationale like a thread being unraveled by some invisible hand.

Somebody walked over, spooking me. I spooked them in return when they realized my car wasn't empty. They quickly retreated inside the restaurant before breakfast ended. The attention I'd craved when I bought the car was becoming a hindrance. I had to get rid of it soon. When I'd pulled up, it elicited "What is he doing eating here?" stares from the underpaid counterpeople. They just didn't know. If I survived this mess, I might find myself telling them to make room behind that register.

Survival.

Can I take your order?

To wake up with the King or to go to sleep with da fishes.

Great choices for someone formerly on the fast track in corporate America.

"Yep. Kash is going to kill me," I affirmed in my mirror. I'd overcome the panic attacks. My encased hand had been steady for the past hour. Maybe I was becoming resigned to my fate.

Still, I didn't want to die.

But my mama didn't raise me for this kind of bleak existence either. I needed to call her. Have that final talk. Tell her I loved her.

My phone vibrated again. I'd tired of the rings through the night. Too many calls, too many debts coming due.

Either Kash or one of his boys, from the number shown. I let the call roll over. Another for the voice mail I'd never check.

I left my car to throw the Burger King bag in the garbage. As I returned, I noticed a black truck as it drove down Forsythe. It looked like any other except for the expensive rims that attracted attention.

Like a pair of diamond earrings on a professional athlete. There I went again—thinking about games.

I couldn't help but laugh. I thought nothing at first as the truck kept moving. Then it slowed, making my heart skip a beat. I almost broke into another panic attack . . . almost pissed all over the fine Italian fibers.

Glad I held my bladder, I watched the truck continue on to its destination. Like that old Geto Boys song I used to jam in college, my mind was playing tricks on me.

I entered my car again, thinking of my next haphazard destination. Eventually, I needed to get to my apartment. Maybe grab some more stuff and run out of town.

The phone vibrated again. Just once this time. Puzzled, I decided to look. Maybe they were giving up.

It was a text message. Three words or three letters . . . if you wanted to call them that. Nonetheless, a message understood: I C U.

He'd found me. I was trembling again, weeping like a baby as the emotions finally overwhelmed me.

I didn't want to die.

I turned the key and my car revved to life. The howl of its engine let me know I was still alive. I mashed the accelerator and sped out of the parking lot, clipping a Corolla as it backed up.

On Forsythe, I instinctively turned against the flow, veering recklessly toward oncoming traffic on the one-way street. In my rearview mirror, I saw three large men scrambling among cars in traffic. The black pickup had pulled over a block away.

They'd just missed me.

Only one person could help me now. And it called for being even less of a man than I'd been lately.

Rock bottom turned out to have another level completely.

I didn't even know if she was home.

But I would wait.

Where was I in a hurry to go?

I wiped my eyes and jumped onto the turnpike.

Please be there, Pumpkin.

24

BIANCA

I remembered seeing an ambulance in the gym's parking lot, but had had no idea. I regretted not walking her out and hoped she would forgive me.

"Try not to disturb her. She had to be sedated," the nurse offered before allowing me to enter. I hated hospitals. Nothing good ever happened there, as far as I was concerned. I offered up a prayer before cracking the door.

I could smell the antiseptic in the air as soon as I entered.

"Hey," Tanner whispered. He was standing at Rory's bedside. He was the one who had reached me with the news. I had just opened my boutique for business when he called. Honestly, the man knew everything that went on in this town. He appeared visibly shaken. I was going to have to be the strong one this time.

Tears filled my eyes as I gazed upon Rory. I'd intentionally avoided looking at my best friend for this very reason when I first entered. A gurgle escaped my throat as I choked up. Tanner came around the bed to hold me. His comfort was uncommon but welcome.

She was so still. An IV was inserted in her arm, the bag dripping medication into her system. Gauze and bandages smothered the top half of her face. Her normal pouty red lips looked pale, dry, and brittle. If she were awake, she would be looking for her lipstick. If she could see it . . .

If she could see.

"Who would do such a thing?" I asked as I wept openly over my friend's condition. "This is evil."

"Couldn't have been a robbery," Tanner replied in his analytical manner. He fought to remove himself from the emotional equation. His way of dealing with it. "They didn't take anything. But why go after her face?"

I lifted my head from his chest and looked toward Rory again. "Not her face," I said. "Her eyes. It looks like they caught her eyes."

"I still think they were trying to ruin her face. Maybe she ducked or turned away."

"Maybe," I said, fixated on the gauze held in place with medical tape. So sad. I walked over and took her limp hand in mine. "Her kids. Has anyone checked on them?"

"Yes. The hospital reached the nanny. She's staying with them. Do you know any of her relatives back in Seattle? They should know."

"No. We never really talked about them. I think her mother's still there."

"Oh," he remarked, fumbling through a difficult moment. He wanted so badly to take charge. "Well, if there's anything your friend needs, I'll pay for it."

I turned to look at this stranger, my eye alight. "That is so sweet of you, dear. You've really surprised me. Thank you."

He just nodded. "I'm going into the hallway. Give you two some time alone."

Rory's hand twitched at the sound of Tanner's voice. A response. With him gone, I tried speaking. Maybe she'd hear subconsciously.

"Rory, it's me. Bianca. Don't worry about a thing. Just get better. Okay?"

The readings on her monitor began jumping. She was probably fighting the drugs.

"Tanner's here too. We just want you to rest. Everything will be all right."

I stroked the back of Rory's hand, trying to soothe her. She began fidgeting. She opened her mouth, trying to speak, but it was slurred and distorted. More sounds than words. Her readings went crazy.

The nurse must've noticed at the monitoring station. She came rushing in, looking concerned, before I had a chance to alert her.

"Ma'am, I'm going to have to ask you to leave. Something has her disturbed. Maybe you should come back later."

"Okay. I'll do that."

Rory's readings spiked as soon as I spoke.

"What's wrong?" I asked the nurse, who'd turned her back to me to administer aid.

"Probably a reaction to the medication. Or maybe she's having a bad dream. Wouldn't be a surprise, considering what happened to her."

I took a final look, then walked out.

Tanner stood outside, talking with a doctor he'd corraled.

"What's wrong?" he asked, seeing the look on my face. The doctor scurried on to his rounds.

"I don't know. I told her I was there and she started freaking out."

"Hmm. Did she say anything?"

"I think she was trying to speak, but I couldn't understand."

Tanner's interest was unusual, but I gave up trying to fathom the workings of his mind. At least he was here rather than holed up in meetings. No time like the present—I proposed something.

"Maybe her kids should stay with us? At least until some of her family can be located."

Tanner's face looked strained. "I don't know if that's such a good idea."

"Why?"

"Why?" he answered with a question. "You know what's happening Wednesday—my appointment to the mayor's committee. And Lorenda's gone, thanks to *whatever* foolishness occurred." His face accused me of that one.

"Yes, but . . ."

He was relentless. Knowing I was on the ropes, he pressed. "And do you have any experience with kids?"

"Well, no. But it's a good idea. Maybe get some practice in for when we—"

He stopped me. "Let it go, Bianca. You know that's a touchy subject."

"I'm sorry. I'm sure we'll be able to one day."

He just shook his head. "Look, I need to get back to the office. Let me get you home first."

"But—"

"You're doing her no good right now. You can always return this evening."

"I need to get back to my job."

"I'm sure that girl . . . um . . ."

"Deonté," I reminded him.

"Yes. I'm sure Deonté is more than capable of running things in your absence."

"And I'm sure your board of directors is more than capable of the same. Come home with me. And stay. Please."

I watched him trying to form a counterpoint. He packed it in early, conceding. "Okay. I need to be there for you. Let's go home. Together."

He kissed me tenderly, then led me to the elevator cradled in his arms.

25

HENRY

After my last time lumbering past the entryway, the doorman began acknowledging my presence . . . and his displeasure with me. I'd lost count of how many times I'd paced the block.

"May I help you?" he asked what must have looked to him like a crazed stalker—disheveled, wrinkled, and in desperate need of a shave.

I didn't answer, poorly pretending that I hadn't heard him and that I hadn't been the same troubled soul he'd been seeing for the past hour. I'd left my wrecked sports car in an alley a few blocks away. I really could use another bottle of Scotch now, but needed to keep my faculties.

For all I knew, Pumpkin may have ended her visit. Gone back to wherever it was that she came from. Maybe she was somewhere whipping that dangerous pussy on another hopeless soul, offering him salvation through his salivation.

I couldn't believe such things. She had to be here. It was just a matter of waiting.

Left with no other choice, I continued my mindless trek, hoping the cops weren't called on me.

It was on another of my passes in front of Pumpkin's apartment. I was trudging with my head down, and carelessly bumped into someone. They quickly brushed themselves off, distancing themselves as if I were a leper. When I turned to offer some words for acting like I was a bum, something else caught my eye. I was suddenly robbed of speech.

A woman walking in the same direction, several yards ahead.

She must've crossed the street behind me. I would've ignored her except that her attire was familiar: the business suit worn by Pumpkin when she gave me the money. It was another sign dropped on my big fat head.

It was her.

It had to be her.

"Pumpkin!" I shouted. She didn't turn around. She was almost a block away. Probably didn't hear me with all the traffic.

Soon she would be out of reach. Behind the golden doors guarded so ferociously by my friend.

I broke out into a full-blown sprint, fueled by the emotions of the moment.

"Pumpkin!" I yelled, a little less desperately this time, as I sprinted through the leisurely gaggle of pedestrians. I could almost reach out and touch her. I was glad I held back.

In my haste, I hadn't noticed that she wasn't alone. She was accompanied by an eerily familiar man. His distinguished gait set him apart. He could've possibly been the brother-in-law she was staying with. The "controlling dick," as I recalled her saying the night I'd pulled her from that car. They were almost to the door. I couldn't waste any more time debating the issue.

I jogged briskly, getting closer, but not attracting attention.

"Pumpkin," I yelled again, to no effect. I debated over grabbing her, deciding I had to do it.

When I touched her shoulder, I knew something was wrong.

The woman flinched at my grip, spinning her shoulder free as if it were something she'd learned in a self-defense class.

"Excuse me?" said the woman wearing the exact same dark green outfit (closer to olive, now that I was seeing it in broad daylight) and with virtually the same measurements as Pumpkin.

Except she wasn't Pumpkin.

Much shorter hair. One of those wavy, sassy styles, but everything else was so . . . similar.

Her sister. It had to be.

"Pumpkin?" I pleaded, knowing it wasn't her, but hoping the mention of her sister's name would alleviate the tension. It was a desperate shot before I resorted to throwing myself at their feet and depending on the kindness of strangers. Blanche DuBois never was in the shit I was in.

Her companion took notice. He stuck his arm out, barring any further interaction between me and Pumpkin's sister. His back was turned, the bum not even worthy of his gaze. He seemed more infuriated with the woman. "You know him?" he asked accusingly.

"I've never seen this man before in my life," she stammered, both frightened and repulsed by me. I forgot how bad I looked . . . and smelled.

Satisfied with the timbre of her answer, he unleashed his disdain on me. Tired of being hit, I defensively raised my cast, expecting a blow. He didn't swing. Just barked as men such as he were apt to do.

"Go away, man," he chastised. "My wife doesn't need this shit."

His voice seemed so familiar. "No disrespect. I just need to see Pumpkin."

"You need to go! We don't know any damn . . . Hold up."

He'd paused with the lowering of my cast from my face. We traded glares, recognition dawning simultaneously. The past twelve hours had made my thinking ragged. It hurt as I tried to fathom what I was in the middle of.

Her sister.

Her brother-in-law.

Tanner Coleman?

"You!" I growled, feeling twelve feet tall before the asshole who had fired me just days ago.

"Henry? What the fuck?" He smiled, but it was one of irritation and annoyance. His wife's weary eyes darted between the two of us, sensing the emotional wave as it came crashing ashore.

What the fuck was this about?

Pumpkin knew. Everything.

Tanner acted before I could dwell on the ins and outs swirling around me. He clamped his hands on my shoulders and tried to throw me. I almost fell over, but held on in return. The two of us spun around in a strange tango until it ended with him slamming me into the brick facade.

"I don't know what kind of sick game you're playing, but you made the worst mistake of your life fucking with me and my wife."

I wasn't his lackey anymore, so I wasn't hearing it. My answer to his indignation was to swing with my cast and hit him upside his pompous head. It dazed Tanner, sending his wife into a shrill shriek. When he staggered back, I tackled the old man. We crashed over a stack of newspapers being sold by a vendor. People on the street awoke from their self-absorption to see two grown men having a midday rumble.

Although older than me, Coleman was quicker and more muscular. A wad of advertisements from Target flew into my face as I brought my cast down in a pounding motion. I missed him as he rolled aside. Before I knew it, he'd grabbed me again, this time wrapping me up in some kind of choke hold. As we tumbled across the papers, I got an elbow into his gut. He broke his grip from around my neck. I hit him upside his head with my cast again, thinking about how I had been willing to kill him a few nights earlier.

Before another blow could be delivered, I was hit from behind. Coleman's trophy wife had run inside, seeking out the inquiring doorman. The young brother had come running and was proceeding to whale on my ass. Coleman had to be a good tipper, because the boy was a zealot, I tell you. He mashed with a ferocity I hadn't seen in Lupe's beat-downs. And I was familiar with those. Once he was sure I was free of his benefactor, he relented, hurling me onto the sidewalk like so much rubbish.

"I knew you were up to something! Now get out of here before I call the cops on your mangy ass!" the doorman yelled as I rose to my feet. He reached down to help Coleman up, but Coleman shrugged him off. He looked perfectly fine. Nothing but a bruised ego.

Police sirens told me this last chance for me was nothing but an illusion. When I was in jail, Kash would be sure to get to me. My immediate choice was simple: I had to flee. As I ran by, I traded looks with Coleman's wife, sensing that something wasn't quite right about her. The uneasy look on her face told me she knew more than she was letting on. Let her have her secrets, then. I would get my answers from her scheming sister.

26

BIANCA

Sure, he'd assaulted Tanner, but our doorman had relished beating that poor soul a little too much. Christ, the man already had a broken hand or something.

He knew Pumpkin—just what no one in this town needed. As he ran by, I couldn't help but feel sorry for whatever she'd gotten him caught up in. It had to be horrible to have reduced him to this. I wondered if the money Pumpkin had stolen had anything to do with his desperate state. With him gone, only one person could provide me with that answer.

"Get away!" Tanner shouted as he shoved Ruben aside. Our doorman was only trying to aid him, but my husband was enraged over the perceived humiliation he'd suffered. "You came out a little late to help. What do we pay you for? What if he'd had a gun?"

A gun.

I hadn't even considered it. And he was so close. I shuddered at what could have happened just now.

After threatening to fire Ruben, Tanner was on a slow burn during the elevator ride up. He looked at me a few times, but backed off without saying anything. He'd been so tender when we left the hospital. Now this unfortunate event had his nostrils flaring.

Opening the door to our place, he let me enter first. The door was barely closed before he erupted. He hurled his keys across the length of the foyer.

"Who the fuck is Pumpkin? Why'd he call you that? Do you know him? Huh? Answer me!"

I shielded my ears from his verbal assault. Instead of running away, I stood my ground and tried to make him listen. "Stop it! Stop! I don't know why he said that!" I barked in response to his accusations. "I don't know that man. Now, please. Stop yelling."

Tanner didn't know her nickname, only her birth name. Revealing that Pumpkin was visiting now would have set him off again. And with all that had happened today, I couldn't take it.

"Are you sure?" he pushed, assuming a more reasonable posture and tone. "Because this motherfucker used to work for me. His name's Harry . . . No. Wait. Henry. That's it. He's the one I fired last week. I told you about that. Are you certain you don't know him?"

"Yes, I'm sure. Tanner, I've never seen that man

before." But Pumpkin had. I was certain. What the hell was she doing?

He analyzed my demeanor as if I were sitting across a boardroom from him, a business ripe for a hostile takeover. His irrational fear of my cheating on him averted, he relaxed and backed down.

"I'm sorry, sweetheart. That man is the last person I expected to come across. Did you see how he looked? So irrational. Almost a completely different person."

"Why did you fire him, again?"

He was pissed that I didn't remember, but indulged me. "He was misappropriating company funds. Over a hundred thousand was being diverted when we caught him. From how he looks, he probably was blowing it up his nose."

"Did you think about maybe getting some treatment for him?"

"No. He's lucky I didn't have him arrested when I threw him out on his bony ass. You don't take what's mine." He grunted, his eyes showing the same faint accusatory trace as before. "What I am going to get is some additional security around this place. Make him think twice about coming around my home."

I sat on our sofa, really taking in how alone I was. Lorenda was gone. Pumpkin may have been lurking in here somewhere, but was wisely hidden. And my best friend . . . my best friend was in the hospital, possibly blinded for life.

Right on time, Tanner wondered aloud, "You think he had something to do with Rory's face?"

I choked on that one. Clearing my throat, I replied, "That's a reach, don't you think? Why would he attack Rory?"

"I don't know. Maybe he'd been stalking me . . . you. Maybe he saw you with Rory. Who knows how long he's been watching us?"

An odd conclusion to come to for sure. My husband seemed utterly paranoid now. Of course, we didn't know who was responsible for Rory's fate. Maybe I was naive.

"Let's not think like that. You're scaring me, Tanner."

He was on his own track, not to be deterred. He hustled over to where he'd thrown his keys and was picking them up. "I'm going to the office. Get some rest, baby. I'm going to look through Henry's personnel file a little more thoroughly. And if I find he did have something to do with hurting your friend, he'll pay."

A shocker that my friend he hardly seemed interested about was consuming more than the bare minimum of his time. Maybe it was all too close to home: Rory's attack, then that man Henry making Tanner feel vulnerable. He needed to channel those feelings of helplessness that the rest of us learn to live with.

He left.

I waited.

Waited for my husband to be stuck in traffic, listening to talk radio en route to his office.

Waited for the silence of my home to suffocate me.

"Pumpkin!" I shouted.

No answer.

The couch was feeling good. Too good for me to get up right now. I groaned. Her not answering didn't mean she wasn't here. It was a big place, and maybe she didn't hear or care to answer. I willed myself to rise and grudgingly went about my sweep of the rooms.

I saved my bedroom for last. Pumpkin seemed to gravitate there. Probably because she knew it unnerved me. Relief enveloped me when I entered my untouched room.

I placed a call to Deonté at the boutique to make sure everything was okay, then called the hospital for an update. No further developments. I decided to rest a little. I would need my strength for when Rory awakened.

Feeling free for the moment, I undressed on the spot, slowly removing my business suit to reveal the results of my workouts. I left my heels on, removing my pants over them. Despite Tanner's actions, I rarely felt sexy. Maybe I should, but it was as though a part of me were missing. I allowed myself to stay in front of the mirror. Curious. The underwear was attractive, matching. My skin was flaw-less. Even my heels weren't bad.

Way too analytical.

I grimaced, wondering if I were turning into a version of Tanner.

As I swiveled, I found myself appreciating the body that filled out my bra and panties. *I do look nice,* I thought to myself. A smile crept across my weary face.

Maybe a little sexy, too.

I struck one of those "come fuck me" poses from the magazines, igniting a sudden feeling of mischie-vousness. *Bad Bianca.*

Since I was ditching it anyway, I unfastened the clasp on the front of my bra. As each cup released, I covered a breast. Just a tease for a pair of imaginary wanting eyes. It felt good visualizing myself this way.

Seeing the beauty for myself rather than through others' eyes.

"Trying to be sexy?" Pumpkin asked. I shrieked, grabbing my bra off the floor to cover myself again.

She'd sneaked up on me, emerging from my walk-in closet. The one place I hadn't checked. Prob-ably trying on my clothes again. *Bitch.*

"You know you can never be me," she teased as she appraised my body, a lollipop dangling from her mouth. When her assessment was finished, she flicked off her shoulders the long black hair atop her head. "Never," she repeated for emphasis.

27

PUMPKIN

"I'd never want to be you," Bianca asserted. Such a liar, that one.

"Keep telling yourself. One day you might believe it. Did I scare you?"

"Yes." She gathered her discarded clothes, quickly grabbing a silk robe off the bed. Her body was nice, but I'd never tell her. "And why are you always in my closet?" she hissed.

"Relax. I was just putting something back. Finally bought some stuff of my own."

"With what?" Bianca asked. "You have nothing. Oh, that's right. You stole from me."

"Don't you think you owe me? After all I've been doing for you?"

"For me? I want you gone, Pumpkin. For good. We just had an incident downstairs with one of your friends. I don't know what kind of chaos you're out there causing. It's scary."

"Oh. Henry."

"I knew it! Yes. Henry."

"I'll set him straight about coming around here unannounced."

"Either do it or Tanner will. Did you know he used to work for him?"

"I may have found out later."

"Did you know he was stealing?"

"Maybe."

"And that doesn't bother you? Oh, that's right. You two are birds of a feather."

"Keep getting flip with me and I'll give you a finger, all right. I said I would set him straight."

"Like you're capable of handling something without messing it up." Bianca laughed.

"I really don't like this new attitude you're trying to sport. While you're trying to *medicate* and sleep your problems away, I'm out here taking care of business. I'm really not the bitch to mess with, so choose your words carefully."

"That's it," she yelled. "I'm telling Tanner all about you. He'll make you leave."

I smirked. Don't know what her doctor had her hopped up on, but she was amusing. I was hungry. *Time to break a few eggs*, as they would say. "Tanner knows I'm here, dumb-ass. And after the visit I had with him the other night, I don't think he'd agree with you." Omelets, if you will.

"You didn't."

"Hey, we're blood. Besides, it's not like I haven't

done it before. Now, your friend, on the other hand . . ."

"Who?"

"The great sightless wonder," I sang. "The overtanned and oversexed blonde."

"Rory . . ." She wept.

"Yep. Tanner's had that. A *bunch*." I chuckled.

"I don't believe you. You're just being evil. Pure evil."

"Never said I was pure, babe. As far as evil, don't think I can top having a child with my wife's best friend. Now . . . *that's* pretty evil. Or a good episode of *Maury Povich*, at the least."

"You're lying." Her jaw trembled. A woman more used to being on the receiving end, she was ready to inflict pain for a change.

"What do I have to do to make you see, Bianca? Do you just tune out everything?"

"Wait. You called her sightless. . . ."

I nodded, a big smile forming as I reflected on my handiwork. "Just looking out for you. Protecting what's yours."

She took a seat on her bed, hands trembling as she clawed at the comforter. She was about to pass out again from the stress of the revelations. Maybe I'd been too harsh. Too much, too soon for such a fragile, delicate mind as hers.

"You are sick. I should call the cops on you," she spat.

I sat next to her. "Go ahead," I whispered in her ear. "Do it. I'll just tell them it was your idea. And who do you think they'll believe? For all they know, I don't even exist."

Bianca lay in the fetal position on the bed, whimpering. A helpless pile of mush. I kissed her on her forehead, telling her it would all work out in the end.

Her phone rang before I had a chance to leave.

"Don't worry. I'll get it."

She didn't reply. Still weeping and rocking atop the pillow-top, a blank stare affixed.

It was the hospital, giving an update on Rory. She was conscious. I gave them a message to take back to her. The nurse seemed disturbed by its contents, but said she'd deliver it. Like I'd told Bianca, I was just protecting what was hers.

I left in search of something suitable to wear. All this crying was making this a depressing place. Maybe it was time to move out.

28

HENRY

I was already missing this town. In one form or another, I knew I was leaving it.

I'd spent the last few hours nursing my wounds from Coleman's pit bull of a doorman.

I was on foot, deprived of the car I'd returned to the dealer, albeit a little banged up. "Send me the bill," I said. An inside joke over their objections and questions.

I strolled, delusional. Almost like I didn't have a care or concern. Ragged and scruffy, I was ignored by the world that used to cater to me. The rumble and raucousness of midday traffic on Tolliver, the corner deli I liked so much on weekends and my occasional day off, the rib joint where I could never get the smell of sauce off my fingers. The aloof Jamaican girl on the third floor whom I should've stepped to.

Instead, I'd rescued Pumpkin on a cold, wet night.

Tanner Coleman's sister-in-law.

And she'd played me. Manipulated me by her words and actions for her own perverse pleasure. I knew she was somewhat off, but loved the rush I felt in her presence. She was unpredictable. A wild card, she'd given me a second chance, even though I'd squandered it on that stupid game.

But still . . . she'd played me. Bad.

Fucking Tanner Coleman.

She knew the whole time. Listening to me gripe and complain while laughing on the inside. Silly me.

I tried suppressing any feelings of gratitude I had for her, exchanging them for the bitterness of the betrayed. If I'd known what I know now, I would've let that car plunge into the river with her in it. I should've never left the parking lot that night. Maybe I should've put that gun to my head, for I couldn't feel any more dead than I did now.

My walk took me to my apartment, where I hoped Kash hadn't left anybody on guard. My intention was to load as much as I could into a suitcase, then leave for parts unknown. I still had my wits and a college degree. Two steps up, as far as I was concerned. As cold as it felt, my heart still beat. I could rebuild.

I was missing my entry key for the front entrance, used to simply driving into the garage. I buzzed, then waited. The manager, a stumpy retiree, shuffled over . . . then paused without opening for me.

I waved at him in his plaid shirt and sweater vest, wondering if his eyes were working. He strained again with his eyes.

"Henry Robinson," I called out. "I left my card upstairs."

That was when I knew how far I'd truly fallen. This man had seen me before, usually speaking in cordial, soft utterances. Now I had to hold up my driver's license to the door to convince him I belonged.

"I'm sorry, Mr. Robinson," he apologized profusely. "You didn't look quite yourself. And these days, you never can be too certain."

"It's all right," I said dismissively, my annoyance obvious. "I don't *feel* quite myself either. Amazing how others see you when you're not *quite* at your best. Something to think about, I guess."

Rather than taking the elevator, I figured I'd err on the side of caution. I found the rarely used stairwell and quickly ascended.

Reaching the fourth floor, I bumped into Mr. Reyes as he exited from my floor above. He wore nothing but a robe and slippers. The scholarly voyeur had a lady friend up there whom he fancied. He seemed embarrassed by my catching him, but I didn't have time for taunts or teasing.

"Good afternoon," he offered as I shoved past him in the tiny confines.

"Hey."

"Um . . . I think you should know—"

"I know, I know. I won't say anything about you and your friend. I'm in a hurry, Mr. Reyes. Talk to you some other time."

"But, wait. There were so—"

I'd already bounded up the last few steps, reaching my floor. "Another time, Mr. Reyes," I yelled down to him. Honestly, the man didn't know when to let it go. He was lucky I didn't get in his face about watching me and Pumpkin that time.

My door was still locked. No break-in or eviction, which was a good sign. I was about to insert my key when something drew my attention. My ears twitched. I had become acclimated to being prey. On the far end of the hall, they appeared. Kash's people. Two of them had chased me outside Burger King. Inside my apartment, I heard footsteps.

Leaving my key in the door, I turned and hauled ass toward the stairs. The large men were faster than I figured. I was overtaken, swept off my feet as if I were a toy. They covered my mouth before I could scream, spiriting me into the gaping jaws of my darkened apartment. The door slammed shut.

"Cleveland. Already in the hole with me . . . and this motherfucker bet on Cleveland." Kash cackled. Against my will, I sat motionless on the floor, my apartment feeling more like a cave in which I was trapped. I'd watched the sun set through my window, unable to enjoy it for even a second. "And with my motherfuckin' money. You're a fuckin' genius, Henry. No wonder you got fired."

The four men thought it funny. They'd tired of chasing me and were looking to work off their stress upside my head. At least they'd waited until Kash arrived with Lupe. That didn't make me feel better. Lupe wasn't smiling tonight. That confirmed that the ride might be over. I imagined a big roll of plastic down in the car that they'd put me on to avoid a mess. I suddenly felt nauseous.

"What's wrong, Henry? Look like you wanna cry. This is gonna cost you. I mean . . . you made it harder on yourself with actin' like a rabbit 'n' all."

"What's harder than death?" I worked up the nerve to say as everything began to crystallize before me.

"The *way* you go out, motherfucker," one of the Burger King Bunch mumbled. He was cleaning his nails as if bored.

"Whatcha got, Henry? Anything up in this apartment in a secret wall safe? Maybe some trust funds or bank accounts? Time's up. Think hard, boy." Kash pulled a chrome-plated memento from his waistband. It emerged, shining, against the backdrop of his ebony attire. My gun. Mine. The irony only appropriate, I suppose.

"I . . . turned my car in. Here. Take my watch.

I . . . I can liquidate some things in here. Or you can just take what you want."

As panicked as I was, I still had a brain. I figured the longer I kept talking, the better my chances were of surviving with maybe just being beaten into a coma. Sometimes people came out of them. Still a gambler, playing those long odds.

"Get up," he said.

I didn't have to be asked twice. My legs were falling asleep anyway. "Please. I don't want to die. C'mon! We go back since high school! Please. Don't do this, man."

The rest laughed at the spectacle. "Punk," came from the nail cleaner. Kash silenced them, my gun still being brandished in his hand.

"I asked you if you had something of value. Maybe make an effort to pay this shit down. You can't think of anything?"

"I already told you what I had." I undid my watch, extended it for him to take. Lupe snatched it instead. "Just give me one last chance."

Six pairs of eyes cast votes in a blink, me in the center awaiting judgment. The rendering came unexpectedly.

Kash sighed. "You do have something of value." I flinched in surprise. "The question is . . . are you willing to deal it . . . or get dealt?"

29

PUMPKIN

"**W**here are you?" I asked when he eventually answered. I didn't like him keeping me waiting. Ruben the doorman was clearing his throat to get my attention, but I shooed him away. I put one finger in my ear so as to hear over the traffic on the street.

"At my place."

"What are you doing there? I thought you were waiting things out at the hotel."

"That's all been solved. Why don't you come by?"

"Can't you pick me up?"

"No. I turned my car in. Catch a cab."

Now he was getting chippy with me. If he was bad as Bianca claimed, then it fit. "Is something wrong with you? My sister told me about what happened."

"I'm sorry about that," he conceded. "Things were a little crazy. It's all good now. Just come by. We'll talk about it."

I agreed to see him, letting him think everything was okay. The man, with his unpredictable nature, could've messed up everything for me. In reality, I was going to give him a piece of my mind, putting him on blast for frightening Bianca. Even if she couldn't fathom my actions, I was protective of her.

A cab stopped without my even whistling, its driver doing that instead as he welcomed me into his dingy yellow transport. I entered cautiously, holding the sides of my skirt.

At Henry's apartment, he plastered me with indifference instead of his usual adulation. Instead of rose petals, his demeanor displayed nothing but thorns. He wore a T-shirt and shorts, as if he'd just showered. I smelled the fresh shower gel lingering in the air.

He left the door open, simply walking away toward the kitchen bar.

I almost walked off, leaving him to his spiral.

His misplaced bitterness toward Tanner was eating him up. Don't get me wrong. A lot of people had reason to hate Tanner, but his hatred was misguided. What the fuck. He got caught stealing. I'd have let him go too . . . if I were responsible and had ethics.

If.

Y'know . . . stupid shit.

"Want some?" He'd downgraded his Scotch for

Wild Turkey, holding the Las Vegas shot glass up in a mock salute. The feeble little man wanted to spar.

"No. Nothing you're offering looks appealing to me anymore," I replied, glaring like the sun. *Burn, little man, burn.*

"I've been hurt worse." He chuckled, wagging his cast about like a fool.

Although he was showered and serviceable, his drooping eyes revealed it to be a ruse for my benefit. He wasn't far removed from the bum described by Bianca. He showed signs of being beaten both physically and mentally, a man worse off than when we rescued each other. It was certain: We no longer shared a life raft. One of us was about to be pushed overboard for the sharks to swallow.

He was too close. He really should have left Bianca alone.

I came closer, knocking the shot glass from his hand. Whiskey doused his face as the glass flew skyward. It clanked off a wall. "What's your problem, Henry? Why'd you come around my sister?" I screamed.

I didn't expect him to break down so fast. His coolness shattered, he lashed out. "I needed some money," he shouted.

"Huh? After what I gave you?"

"Yes. I messed up, like I always do. Didn't realize it was coming from Tanner Coleman, though.

Your fucking brother-in-law. Big surprise, Pumpkin. Thanks."

There. He got it out.

"And? You planned on robbing him that night, Henry. I just did you one better. Now you have the nerve to be mad at me? When I tried helping you?"

"Help? Help? Maybe help yourself by fucking with my head, you crazy bitch."

"You want to cast judgment? Well, I can too. You are spineless and soft. But worst of all . . . you're weak, Henry. Help. Yeah, I was trying to help you. For real. But you're too pathetic to realize it. Now . . . who's the bitch?"

Applause rang out, startling me.

I was so angry that I'd let my guard down. I was the one swimming with sharks.

The two thugs from the Radisson came out of Henry's bedroom. Two more had come in through the front door, blocking it. *What have you done?* my expression asked. He sat on the couch and sighed, afraid to look at me.

"Yeah, bitch. You're right. Henry is pathetic," the chocolate one crowed. "Pathetic enough to give you up."

30

HENRY

No more.

No more broken bones and threats of pain or death. I took the offer made by Kash, a sure bet even to one with my unfortunate luck. When faced with the alternative, it came easily.

And all I had to do was give her up.

Not as easy as I thought.

I'm sorry, Pumpkin.

"Henry," she called out as Kash and his crew shuffled toward us. I lowered my head, too embarrassed to face her.

"Henry ain't who you need to be talking to. Your salvation lies in me," Kash teased. He opened his arms as if she were to seek a hug from him.

"Fuck you," she spat defiantly. Unafraid, yet troubled by what was registering, she quizzed me again. "Is this true? Did you set me up, Henry? I'm supposed to help bail your ass out again?"

She still wasn't getting it. They didn't know the

money had come from her before. Kash liked what he saw that night at the Radisson.

She was to be the payoff.

I looked at her and spoke. "I . . . I'm so sorry," I whimpered.

"No. Oh, no," she repeated, shaking her head. The four of them closed in, their lust growing. One of the men removed his black sweatshirt over his head, exposing a soft, round gut. The other snickered at the sight, but began undoing his belt.

"Maybe if you give them some money they'll back off, Pumpkin," I blurted out in desperation.

"That was a onetime deal. Fuck them, and fuck you, Henry!"

"*Fuck us?*" Kash mocked, feigning indignation. They all laughed, hearty growls echoing off the burgundy walls. "Now we're getting down to business."

Lupe went to grab her by the arm. She slapped his hand hard enough to leave a mark. He backed off, deferring to Kash, although he clearly wanted to hit her.

"I like feisty. But it ain't gonna save ya."

Pumpkin did a quick spin, then backed up, moving away from the loose circle that had formed. Ever defiant, she assessed things, then did the unexpected.

Seeming suddenly resigned, she sighed. "Damn. You want me that bad? I should be flattered."

Kash and the rest didn't know what to say. Didn't expect Pumpkin to back down. Now that she was less of a threat to them, the shirtless one with a gut began scurrying to get his jeans off.

She removed the sleeveless designer tee, the skin of her toned midriff exposed first, then her perfect breasts. Kash grunted approvingly. "Now that's what I'm talkin' 'bout, baby."

I watched, still afraid of doing something but also afraid of what was to come.

With a firm tug, she pulled the denim skirt off. It slid down her legs until she stood there in nothing but a thong and heels. I was never in more fear, yet equal awe.

There was an eerie pause.

"Who's first? Don't be shy now," Pumpkin encouraged.

Two of Kash's men got into a shoving match, each wanting to be the first to smash the pumpkin. They were almost to blows when Kash put an end to it.

"Get to the back of the line," he ordered. "I'm taking this for a ride first."

"Think you can handle the ride, Kash? Or am I gonna have you crying like Henry?"

They all laughed at the entertainment. She lied, though. I never cried.

"I ain't a punk like Henry. Best believe." Kash rubbed his hands together as if about to feast on prime rib. Pumpkin didn't shrink away as he came closer. She just smiled. Ever dangerous and unpredictable.

He put his hands on her ass, taking a firm grip as he probably salivated. She swiveled her hips as he held on. He almost had a fit.

"Oh, shit," he squealed. "Sorry, Henry, but we about to take this to the bedroom."

The remaining three, Lupe included, began throwing their clothes off at his proclamation.

"Not without a kiss first."

"Say what? I don't do that kissin' stuff. But don't worry. Once I put this dick in you, you'll forget about that."

She folded her arms, pouting. She whipped her head about, sending her long black strands dancing. "No kiss . . . none of this."

"I'll kiss her! And that too!" Mr. Belly howled. Kash scowled at him.

The big man gave in, closing his eyes as he puckered. Amazing how easily she got men to act so childlike.

Pumpkin leaned over toward his lips, the whole room hinging on what was going to be a feeding frenzy. I was repulsed, wanting to turn away, but fixated as she . . .

Jabbed a thumb in his eye.

"Aaaaaaaaah!" Kash shrieked. As his hand went up, Pumpkin kneed him between the legs. He doubled over once his body realized what had just happened. I hadn't grasped it, but she'd backed up to that particular spot on purpose. To her left was an antique vase on display. I'd bought it on vacation in Italy a few years ago. She was already pivoting toward it as Kash's head dipped. In a fluid motion, she snatched it up and brought it smashing against the side of his head. As he fell down, Pumpkin assisted him with a shove, breaking into a full-on sprint for the front door.

"Bitch," Kash screamed in a garbled manner.

Lupe, down to his underwear, had to leap across the couch. She got her hand on the door just as he caught her, yanking her away from freedom.

She was about to swing on him if not for the vicious backhand he delivered first, lifting her off her feet. Her hair swirled across her face as her body tumbled away. As the ebon strands turned, they did something funny. They took on a life of their own, going over her now swollen cheek then across her nose and face. They continued . . . airborne.

The mass of hair flew through the air until landing by my shoulder. Almost alive, like a giant spider.

No.

A wig.

I was stunned.

Pumpkin grabbed her face, recovering from the

recoil. Her breathing was labored as she righted her-self. Lupe prepared to hit her again, but she wasn't fighting anymore.

Just standing there . . . wobbly. And possessing short, wavy hair.

The same hair I'd seen earlier on her . . .

Sister.

Lord, no.

She looked around the room as if it were the first time she'd been here. Lupe was spooked. Kash was being attended to by his boys, but she never made another effort to escape. When she turned in my di-rection, she stopped. I stood up despite the conse-quences, concerned for someone other than myself for a change. Her eyes were glazed, trancelike.

Then she blinked.

And I saw her eyes didn't match. Well, not really her eyes as much as the colors of her pupils. Lupe's blow had not only knocked the wig off; it had jarred loose a contact. A colored contact.

The eyes rolled back as if she were about to faint. I took a step toward her, but she righted herself.

She looked at me again, but she was differ-ent. The posture and defiant demeanor had been replaced. Shoulders sunk, defeated and unsure. Realizing she was nearly nude, she brought her hands over her breasts as if suddenly modest. She began mumbling something, but it sounded like gibberish.

This was a different person looking at me.

"You! What am I doing here? What did you do to me?" The woman gasped, pointing an accusing finger at me before she screamed.

It couldn't be. Yet it was.

Lupe shook off his surprise and grabbed her in a bear hug, covering her mouth with his hand. As he carried her away, she flailed and kicked violently. Kash motioned for him to bring her to the bedroom, where no one would hear her.

"Bitch about to get it," he cursed, charging right behind them. The others eagerly followed, leaving me by myself. My bedroom door slammed shut, but it didn't muffle the sounds of sobbing and pleading.

I heard the crack of a slap. Probably Kash getting his revenge.

Pumpkin was Tanner Coleman's wife.

I tried to fathom the revelation, but it was hard to accept. Nearly impossible.

But there was the proof. A simple wig and colored contacts.

"No! Please!" came from my bedroom, jolting me out of my contemplation.

Whoever that woman was, she didn't deserve this. God forgive me, what had I done?

I had to stop this, further injury to myself be damned.

I built up a head of steam before launching myself into the bedroom door. Nobody was blocking it, so it popped open.

On my bed, on my beautiful bed, was a scene of terror.

Coleman's wife was clawing at the sheets, whimpering, while Kash proceeded to rape her. Each sob was met with a brutal, unforgiving thrust between her legs. One of the men had pinned her hands down. He gave me a nod, as if to say I could have a turn when they were finished.

"Stop! I messed up. You don't know who that is. This is a big mistake," I pleaded. "I'll get your money. Just leave now before this shit gets worse."

"Too late, boy," Kash huffed, sweat already forming. "We're going to be here a looong time."

Beneath him, she'd heard me and reacted. "Please. Help me," she gasped. Her eyes screamed at over one hundred decibels. I'll never forget that look as long as I live.

I ran toward the bed before they could stop me. I tried grabbing Kash to pull him away. We struggled until he got a hand in my face. As he pushed my head back, he was holding it steady for Lupe.

His right-hand man rocked me with a punch so hard that my ears rang and one of my crowns popped out of my mouth. I crumpled off Kash as fast as the clothes he'd shed. I wasn't on the floor long before being dragged to my closet, where I was beaten down and dumped.

As I lay there in the dark, semiconscious, I was forced to endure the screams and struggles as they took their turns with Coleman's wife. As she wept, I wept for her. Too weak when I needed to be strong—the story of my life. I don't know how long I was in there, but could sense when she'd given up, her spirit broken. I must have passed out, for all of sudden the closet door was yanked open. Light overloaded my senses as a pair of hands yanked me to my feet.

Coleman's wife was still in my bed as I emerged from the closet. Most of the bedding was ripped off except for the thin sheet wrapped around her body. She was alive, but silent. That was all I could see as I was quickly ushered to the living room. An audience with Kash.

Kash was putting on his clothes, squinting still from the thumb poke. The rest of them pranced around as if they'd just participated in some great sporting event. Sick fucks.

"Henry, you all right?" he asked, snapping his fingers as if bringing me out of a trance. I just stared, wondering how successful I'd be if I took another shot at him.

"We're done now. So get the fuck up out of my apartment," I growled. My jaw was sore.

"I think I knocked something loose in his head." Lupe chuckled. Damn, he could hit.

"Yeah, I think you did, bro. Otherwise Henry

would know better than to ask for another ass whippin'. Oh . . . and Henry?"

"Yes?" I said dryly.

"We ain't over."

"Yeah. We are," I corrected him. "You said—"

"Said what?" he cut me off, indignant. "You thought your whole debt was erased by that? You thought that crazy piece of pussy in your bedroom was worth a couple hundred grand? It wasn't even that good. Besides, I only fuck with long-hair bitches. Didn't know that was a wig when I first met her."

"C'mon, man. Let this shit go. This has gotten out of hand."

Now that his shoes were on, he rose. Patted me on my shoulder as if imparting great wisdom.

"Relax, boy. I ain't gonna fuck you up this time. Consider that in there as a down payment on your tab. Now clean this mess up and get some rest. Let your hand heal. Eat some food; get your strength back. Maybe get a gym membership. Put a little meat on those ribs."

They began leaving, Kash whistling as he strolled away from me.

"Why? What the fuck does that mean?"

"You're going to work the rest of your tab off for some of my clients with . . . um . . . different tastes." His crew thought it funny. I didn't. "Don't worry. They pay well. You'll be done after a few years or so. Your jaw and asshole might be used to it after the first couple of months. Who knows? You might even come to like it."

They laughed heartily on that note, closing the door behind them. I ran and locked it, in case they returned, before going to check on Coleman's wife.

31

BIANCA

"What do you remember?" Tanner asked.

In the backseat, he held me, rocking back and forth all the while. My face was cradled next to his cast. The strange man named Henry.

"I'm sorry. I'm so sorry," he kept repeating as if it were a prayer. I didn't want him touching me, but was too numb to do anything. The man who was driving reminded me of one of those Ivy League academics. I kept hearing his small dog barking. Wondered what breed it was.

"I figured it out but couldn't tell them who you were," he confessed, thinking I was too far gone to be listening. I think he was crying. "They would've killed you when they were through rather than face that kind of heat. You have to believe me when I say I'm sorry. I didn't know."

They'd brought me here to Saint Aloysius, abandoning me in the emergency room before fleeing into the night. I don't remember much after that. I wish I'd forgotten what happened before.

The four of them hovering over me, laughing. Each one taking his turn forcing himself inside me, ignoring my screams and pleas to stop. I think they enjoyed my terror more than the act. The one in charge, his foul breath and crooked smile. The things he said as he . . .

What would Tanner think?

I'm ashamed that I was concerned about such a thing.

"What do you remember?" Tanner repeated. My eyes darted between the doctor and him. A silent plea went out. She sensed my discomfort.

"Mr. Coleman, could you leave us for a moment?" the soft-spoken Asian woman requested. "I need to complete my exam."

"If it's okay with my wife, I'll leave. Otherwise . . ."

"It's okay, Tanner. I'll be fine." I patted his hand on my shoulder, feigning reassurance when in reality I was terrified.

A scared little girl. Again.

My husband reluctantly obliged, leaving to meet with the police detectives and possible media. My body ached so much, but it was troubling how *missing* I felt, if that made any sense. In a strange bedroom, they'd killed something inside me spiritually. I had no idea how I'd gotten there or why they would do such a thing. I just knew they were evil men.

My throat hurt from crying, yet I broke down again.

"We're almost finished, Mrs. Coleman. I know this can be difficult with your husband here." She rubbed my arm reassuringly.

"Yes. It is."

"Did you know the people who did this? In most cases, it's someone familiar to the victim."

I'm sorry, he kept saying.

"No. I don't know them. Never saw them before in my life." I stared into the blackness of the hospital window. In its reflection, I saw what had been replaying through my mind again and again. I shut my eyes to block it out.

"Well, the police are going to want a few minutes with you. Evidence preservation. Whenever you're comfortable. Maybe they'll put these animals behind bars."

She left me alone. From behind the curtain dividing the examination room, I expected the monsters to return. I wasn't sure if I could endure describing my ordeal to the police.

"Bianca? Baby?" They came as whispers, but were forceful in their clip.

Tanner had returned. I could've pretended to be asleep, but he would have persisted. His ego demanded answers.

Answers that, frankly, I didn't have.

"Hey, honey." I sighed, posing as if resting.

He checked the examination room, peeking behind the curtain. I felt relieved the monsters weren't there. "The police will be here soon. I wanted to get in here first. Make sure you're okay."

"Okay?"

"Well . . . that you're not any worse."

"I'm just happy you're here, baby."

"I have to ask you, Bianca . . ."

"Yes?"

"Do you know the people who did this?"

"The doctor just asked me that."

"And?"

I gulped; it was difficult to swallow. He saw me reaching for some water and handed the cup to me. "No," I answered after taking a sip and clearing my throat.

"Where were you, anyway? How did these guys get hold of you? I had extra security at our place. And no one saw you leaving."

"Tanner . . . I don't remember."

He pondered. "Hmm. Maybe they broke in and drugged you. I'll have the locks checked. Lorenda had keys. I certainly hope she didn't get hooked up with someone meaning to do me harm."

"You?"

"Well . . . you know. Get at me through you."

He may have had a point. Still, his questions and

accusations wore on me. I wished he'd stop. Maybe the police would arrive soon.

"This is too much of a coincidence. All this stuff happening days before the mayor appoints me. Rory, Henry outside our apartment, and now this. It just seems orchestrated. And it doesn't look good to have scandal swirling around the Coleman name. I need to get to the bottom of this and make whoever's responsible pay."

I struggled to sit up. "Isn't that the job of the police?"

"At times," he muttered, eyes suddenly icy. The only face I had recognized was that man Henry. As weird as it seemed, something told me not to share that with Tanner. When the police arrived, I didn't know if I'd be so hesitant.

"Mrs. Coleman?" the doctor announced, returning to check on me. "If it's okay, the detective would like to speak with you."

I'm sorry. I'm so sorry, Henry had said in the car.

"I'm ready to speak with them," I answered.

32

PUMPKIN

All those questions they had for Bianca. Poor thing had no answers—only humiliation and pain. Between the police and Tanner, they'd pounded away until she'd fallen asleep. I was exposed, and poor Bianca had to suffer for my mess-up. Damn her for not allowing me to reassert control when that was happening.

I hoped her dreams were peaceful, for I was about to make life for some a living hell.

The IV had done me some good, but a big, fat hamburger was on my mind. A meat eater I was. And I hated hunting on an empty stomach.

Bianca was being held for observation, but I wasn't one for being watched. I had places to go.

I pulled out the needle and yanked the bandages off my arm.

Lowering myself to the floor, I limped over to the restroom, legs a little wobbly after what those little-dick motherfuckers had attempted to do. It wasn't about rape. They tried to break a bitch. Thing is, they didn't get it done.

Sure, I was a little banged up, but my face was in pretty good shape. Hated the look, but I would have to suffer through it until I got my hair and eyes back. Upon further thought, my current look still had some use.

"I need you to get my doctor now!" I screamed frantically as I staggered into the hallway.

"Mrs. Coleman, I'm under orders to stay here."

"And I'm ordering you to get my doctor. Please. I just had a bad dream. And . . . and . . . I can't take it." I put my face in my hands and began sobbing.

I hated using Bianca, but it didn't take a lot to fake the weak-sister act. The security guard bit on it, dashing down the hall to get my doctor. I removed my hands from my dry face, exiting in the opposite direction in search of something more stylish than the drab, ill-fitting hospital gown.

So much destruction, so little time. I sighed as I sauntered by the empty nurses' station.

The cab dropped me off eight blocks away. I walked the rest after questioning the manhood of my Pakistani driver and shorting him ten bucks. Even though my destination was in the heart of Hunter's Green, I wasn't staying away. I stood across the street, watching. Blending in below the broken streetlight amidst the crackheads and other quick studies of life's inequities.

They were afraid to walk on *that* side of Crawford Street. In front of the house that didn't quite blend in—the front yard way too clean, burglar bars and a security camera, the new trucks in the driveway no one would dare touch. It spoke to me.

Money.

Cash money.

Kash money.

The inside of the house probably resembled a touch of Henry's upscale loft with a dash of the TV show *Good Times*.

Unfortunately, I didn't get the memo to be afraid.

Tonight.

Tonight it was going down.

A man like Kash made enough from suckers like Henry to live on the same block as Tanner. But he was all about keeping it real.

The fool.

Wrong time for that. Made me think about that *Chappelle's Show* skit "When Keepin' It Real Goes Wrong."

A porch light came on, drawing my interest. The bright Hispanic flunky emerged in his underwear, throwing out some boxes of Popeyes chicken. Made me regret the burger I'd had. After he discarded the trash in the garbage can, he brushed off his hands.

The casual manner in which he acted broke it down for me. The hood was their comfort zone. Everywhere else, they had to have their guard up. Here, they understood the game and felt safe.

Before he returned to the house, he pushed the remote on the black Yukon. Once it unlocked, its lights came on. He was reaching underneath the front seat when I sneaked up. I feared it was a gun he was going for, so I had to be quick.

As he exited, he saw my smiling image in the door mirror and froze. A ghost, he had to think, considering what he and his friends had done to Bianca.

Except the ghosts I knew didn't pack old screwdrivers. Amazing what you can find on the sidewalks on this side of town.

Silly man would've agreed if he weren't collapsing with it stuck in his neck.

As he went down, he reached for me, snagging my arm, his other hand desperately covering the fatal wound in his neck. I spat on him as his grip slowly diminished.

I stood over him, observing the life fade from his eyes, remembering the silent curse I'd made as he took his turn with Bianca. When I was powerless.

I placed my foot atop his chest.

"Good night," I said smartly with a wave as he made his final gasp.

Curious whether I might find a better weapon

to use, I reached into the Yukon to retrieve whatever he'd been going for.

A bottle of K-Y. The kind that warmed. Good choice, but not a weapon unless one was wielding a slippery dick.

No wonder none of the fellas were hanging outside tonight. Entertainment was going on inside.

Cautiously entering the open door, I expected someone else to be on guard.

Nobody.

Even the stairs descending to the basement were dark and still. Instead I spied numerous notebooks and ledgers stacked neatly throughout in enormous columns as far as the eye could see. Kash hadn't gotten with the digital age, relying on whatever wits he'd inherited instead of a formal education. I assumed the records were organized according to some system—between small fish and big suckers like Henry. Probably other types of business mixed in to diversify his criminal portfolio. A man like that could've been valuable to Tanner.

Oh, well. Maybe in the afterlife. They both deserved a hell.

"Lupe?"

I bristled at the sound of the voice, ducking against a stack of notebooks that slid over. Whoever it was stopped, sensing they weren't alone.

"Lupe, Kash said to hurry up," came from innocent vocal cords for which I wasn't prepared.

I stepped out from my vantage point to confront the young girl. I wasn't expecting Kash to have his kid in this environment.

Except it wasn't his kid.

Damn.

Kid was about thirteen in spite of the attitude she tried to project. She wore only a T-shirt, one adorned with one of those sassy slogans that seemed inappropriate for her age. I was the last one to be acting motherly, but . . .

"Go. Now. And don't come back," I said sternly. "Or I will find you and beat your little ass."

She nodded, agreeing before darting past me. I don't know if she saw the body outside, but she'd probably seen worse growing up around here.

A TV was on toward the rear of the house, just past the kitchen. Sounded like somebody had a porno on. Just the way to relax after a gang rape, I guess.

"Lupe, hurry the fuck up! This little bitch gotta be home soon." Kash's throaty voice bellowed. I followed the sound. And my palms began sweating.

In the kitchen was a bank of monitors connected to the exterior cameras. No one was minding them. Careless.

Atop one of them rested an expensive watch—someone's collateral. Its familiarity led me to pick it up.

"Henry," I muttered upon closer inspection. I

stowed it in my pocket, knowing I didn't have time to dwell on such things. Kash would become curious sooner or later.

"Money, what you doin' in there?" He'd heard my shuffling around, but was too lazy to get up.

"Nothin'," I answered as close to her adolescent voice as I could.

"Where's Lupe?"

"He on the phone."

"Oh. Well, get your ass in here then."

Kash didn't react when my hand reached in and flipped off the light switch. He was still bathed in the unflattering light of *Black Orgy Jam IV*. He was drunk and fixated enough on the on-screen ass slapping to miss that the nude girl in his bedroom was several inches taller than Money. Lying there unclothed, he held a lit cigar in one hand and a half-full bottle of vodka in the other, making a mess of himself.

Then he saw the silhouette of my breasts.

"Damn, them things grew?"

"Uh-huh," I whispered as I clung to the wall, easing closer.

"Come here! Let me suck on them!" he squealed, his vision blurry enough to grant me more time.

I sprang quickly, straddling him as I brought something onto the bed with me. I fought the urge to throw up, being this close. He reached up to grab my breasts at the same time he tried to push that dick in me again. I squirmed away, pinning down his arms and moving up his body until my pussy was in his face.

I rose onto my feet on the bed, allowing me to squat just above his mouth. As I thought, he couldn't take his eyes off it. Just dancing there, mesmerizing him. He tried to lap at it with his tongue, but it was just out of reach. He tried one more time and I moved away accordingly. He grinned, enjoying the tease. He focused on my pussy again, this time squinting through the haze. As drunk as he was, even he wasn't blind.

"You got some hair on that. That ain't a little girl's. Damn, that looks like a woman's—"

"You know what I did wrong before?" I pondered in my own voice, cutting him off. "I didn't hit you hard enough with that vase."

Kash's eyes widened to where I could see them in the darkened room. That lasted just until I brought the black cast-iron skillet from the kitchen over my head. I gave in to gravity, bringing it down upon his skull with a crack and a splatter of blood.

On reflex, he jabbed with his cigar, burning me on my side with the tip until I smacked him with the skillet again.

Then both his flailing arms fell lifeless at his side.

I was clothed when he regained a semblance of consciousness. Being awake but with no mobility must've have been frightening to a man such as him. Freak that he was, there were several tools of bondage in his basement. I'd dug around, taking the time to cuff his wrists to the bed. I nudged the mattress with my foot, impatient with his progress. I was on a schedule.

When that didn't move him along fast enough, I filled the same skillet I'd wielded with water and poured it on his face. He gasped to life, eyes enraged.

"Do you know the shit that comes out of your mouth when you're dreaming?"

"I'ma kill you," he snarled. "Lupe!"

"Lupe's dead," I dryly proclaimed. "Want to guess who's next?"

He tried to lunge at me. His body, slowed from the blow to his head, came to an abrupt halt when his cuffs reached their limits. I watched his body spasm, then fall back onto the bed. Amusing.

He went with another strategy.

"Look . . . I'm sorry. I'll give you whatever you want. I've got lots of money. Just let me go. All right?"

"You can't give me anything. But you did take something from someone I love."

"Henry?"

"No. Bianca."

"Who?" he remarked. "Who the fuck's Bianca?"

"Never mind. Don't worry your head over such

matters." I leaned over, kissing the large naked man on his forehead, just to the side of the deep bleeding gash I'd made. He tried grabbing me with the closest hand, but I backed off too quickly.

I picked up a batch of tablets I'd gathered. Lists of bets, lists of debts. I ripped a few pages out, sprinkling them over the bed.

"What the fuck are you doing? I need those!"

He still didn't get it. I didn't answer, leaving the low hissing sound from the kitchen to greet his ears.

"Wait. Wait. What's that smell?"

I tore out several more pages, repeating the step. A final sheet, showing the mind-boggling amount owed by Henry, I rolled up into a semitube. Kash's still-lit cigar was used to ignite it. As the paper fed the flames, blackness rolling over the field of college-ruled white, I took a drag.

Exhaling a cloud of sweet smoke, I answered, "I think that smell is barbecue."

I dropped the sheet of paper, now fully engulfed, onto the bed, where the fire began to spread. Kash kicked frantically, succeeding in knocking the flaming records onto the floor, but I'd already encircled the bed with several torn tablets before he awoke. He'd just given the flames more fuel.

"Let me go! Please!" he screamed as he thrashed about wildly. Still the cuffs held. Similar cries had been made by someone earlier that night. And like his, they had fallen on deaf ears.

My answer was a smile. "In your next life, be careful who you fuck with," I offered in parting.

He began shouting at the top of his lungs. Nobody was coming, though. Ironic. The same thing that allowed him to operate in this neighborhood untouched would allow me to walk away just the same with no witnesses.

He'd be left here to panic . . . and burn . . . then die. Alone.

The escaping gas from the line I'd ruptured in the kitchen was bordering on overwhelming. Coughing, I quickly exited Kash's lair.

I stood across the street again, witnessing the billowing smoke with the gathering crowd. Over the murmur, I imagined hearing Kash's screams.

Then it erupted.

An all-consuming ball of fire as the windows on his place exploded. The roof disintegrated, dropping its flaming remnants all across the yard and driveway.

Some of the crowd backed off to safer positions, fearing a larger explosion. The warmth of my creation was soothing in the biting night air. I stood my ground until I was sure the monster was consumed.

"Godzilla ain't got nothin' on me," I joked to myself.

As the fire trucks began arriving, I took my leave.

33

HENRY

My apartment.

A dwelling like anyone else's.

A smashed vase. Pillows overturned. Scuff marks on the hardwood floors. A cigarette extinguished with somebody's foot. And the smell that permeated everything no matter how many windows I opened to the frigid night air.

A dwelling like no other.

The symbol of my ascendancy in life was now a mark of shame and sorrow. The place felt used . . . or misused, more accurately. A large, festering sore of how low I'd sunk. I could no longer enter my own bedroom, knowing what I'd allowed to go down.

Pumpkin was Tanner's wife.

No matter how many times I repeated it in my head, I couldn't accept it.

After Mr. Reyes helped me bring her to the hospital, I'd remained seated on the couch. Same place I'd sat like a good little lapdog for Kash.

Dog. Bitch. Interchangeable as far as the definition applied to me.

Being fucked so much, somewhere along the way, I'd forgotten how to be a man.

I could've run, like I planned to initially. Kash and his boys would be gone awhile. Plenty of time to make my escape.

Instead I waited for the police to come and arrest me.

"Mr. Reyes, I appreciate your help, but you have to go now. I don't want you getting in any trouble on my account."

"Uh . . . I can stay around, Henry. Really. I saw those men prowling outside your door. I could tell the police that you tried to stop them. You did try to stop them . . . right?"

My cast was beginning to itch. I'd just noticed. I banged it on the edge of the coffee table.

"Right?" he asked again.

"Yeah. I guess."

"Okay," he said with a sigh. He didn't say it, but my stature in his eyes was diminished . . . tarnished. "Well, I've read up on these sorts of things. You can get a lawyer and—"

"Really. It's okay. I'll face whatever's coming alone. Thank you. It's been . . . nice having you as a neighbor." I stuck out my good hand, waiting for him to shake.

This was a debate he didn't want to engage in.

"I see," he said.

We shook; then he left with his Yorkie under arm.

Time elapsed as I sat there, all silent except for the tick-tock of my clock. No police sirens. No knock at the door. Not even the shuffle of footsteps in the hall.

They weren't coming for me. At a moment when I prayed not to be alone . . . not even the cops would honor my desires.

"Damn," was all I could summon in the end.

What Kash had in mind for me, I knew I couldn't do. I got up, steeling myself for what I'd come to do originally when I came back: Grab some shit and run.

I made my visit to the bedroom a short one, grabbing whatever I could add to my already over-filled bag. I took the sheets, as awful as they were, off the bed and rolled them up into a ball. I would toss them in the Dumpster downstairs. When I got to the bus terminal, I would be on the first thing leaving town.

I cast a backward glance, flipping the light off a final time. But turning it off wouldn't turn off her screams. Pumpkin or whoever the fuck she was. Like her lovin', good mornings were in my rearview mirror.

My eyes blurred as I left the bedroom. I clenched my teeth in an effort to fight back tears. I wiped the one that escaped as I opened my apartment door.

"Boo."

"Ahhh!" I yelped, jumping back over the threshold.

Heart racing, I dared looking into the abyss that was my apartment hallway.

And the abyss looked back.

There she was. Really.

Not a figment of a guilty conscience.

It wasn't the woman I'd left at the hospital.

Don't ask me how I knew. I just did.

"Running somewhere, you piece of shit?"

I dropped my bag as well as the sheets I was to dispose of. I wanted to grab her in my arms, tell her how glad I was to see her. And how sorry I was for what I'd done. Instead I stood frozen, unsure of what would be appropriate.

She came in, a feat of incredible strength on her part. I don't know how she was able to function. Other than looking exhausted and cold, the woman seemed healthy. While that was the physical aspect, the mental was seriously in question.

"I was leaving. For good."

She saw the wig on the floor. I hadn't touched it. She bent over, picking it up and inspecting it curiously. Satisfied, she then affixed it without missing a beat. When she turned to me again, I saw the dried blood on her face. As she took one step forward, I did the opposite. She smiled.

"Maybe you should've been scared sooner," she growled. No purr in the kitten.

"I tried to stop it. Believe me, Pump—" I caught myself. "Who are you? I mean . . . really."

"Does it matter?"

"Yes. It does."

"Maybe before." She sighed. "But you fucked that up. It's over, Henry. I just came to bring you something."

"Huh?"

She reached in her pocket. When I saw something glistening, I flinched. It was too small to be a gun, though. She threw it up in the air.

I snagged my watch, realizing the implications of how she'd gotten it.

"No need to run. Your debt is canceled. That fat piece of shit won't be bothering you anymore," she huffed.

"No way. I don't believe it."

"Go see for yourself. Dead men tell no tales. And ghosts can't hurt you. At least, yours can't." Her eyes gleamed at the end. Just before she turned to leave.

"Wait." She paused. "Thank you," I said, daring to touch her shoulder.

She kept her eyes fixed on her exit. I wished she'd looked at me, allowed me to atone somehow. In that moment, I knew that I no longer cared that she was Tanner Coleman's wife or what her actual name was. I wanted to take that final gamble—that

I could turn myself around and make her proud of me. That I could be her man, in deeds rather than mere ethereal words.

"Henry?"

"Yes," I answered, hoping.

"One other thing," she commented as she glared at my hand. "If I ever see you again, I'll kill you."

My hand was still there.

But the shoulder on which it had rested was gone.

Good-bye, Pumpkin.

34

BIANCA

The last thing I remembered was being at the hospital, beaten . . . violated. And questioned unmercifully by the police. On the face of the male officer, I read his unspoken accusations.

You must've done something to be in this predicament.

You had to know those men.

What really happened?

And why aren't you telling us where you were? Probably somewhere you shouldn't have been. Little Miss High Society went looking for some excitement and things got out of hand?

Are you on drugs? Are you selling your body for a high?

We'll find out. So you might as well tell us now.

I was glad when the medication granted me solace.

Now I was home. Bathed and resting peacefully in my bed. With no clue how'd I gotten here.

And losing my mind, so it appeared.

"Bianca!"

My husband's scream carried from the front door to the third floor, commanding me to attention. Had he brought me home? What they gave me at the hospital must've been strong.

Another mystery before me as I struggled to rise from the bed. Tanner sounded enraged. Maybe he'd found out about that man Henry's involvement. And about how I'd kept that fact from him and the police.

Worse. Maybe he knew Pumpkin was here. Time to 'fess up after all that had occurred.

On wobbly legs, I fetched my robe and strode in search of what had Tanner so distressed.

"Bianca!" he shouted again. I peered over the banister, observing him pacing recklessly over the Persian rug he rarely stepped on. "Get your ass down here! I know you're home!"

I scurried down the stairs as fast as I could, not looking forward to the storm brewing below. "Tanner, why are you screaming at me?" I asked.

His eyes rolled. Indignation at my having the gall to ask such a thing. And a brief respite for me before he unloaded.

"Where the hell did you go?"

"I honestly don't know. I just woke up in my bed."

"Bullshit! You need to quit with the amnesia act and be straight with me!" He charged me as if to strike before backing away into his frenetic pacing again. After a deep breath, he erupted once more. "The guard at Saint Aloysius said you diverted his attention, then disappeared. I've been combing the city for fear that you were lying dead in some alley or something. Then . . . then while I'm in the limo, I get a call from the hospital where Rory's staying. They claim you left a harsh message for her that has her climbing the walls. By this point, I'm losing my mind. Then I get here and that doorman Ruben says something about seeing your sister, but not you. I fired the stupid retard on the spot! You don't have a fucking sister, Bianca! Now what the hell's going on?"

"It . . . it's Pumpkin," I stammered as I tried to catch my breath. "Pumpkin's responsible for a lot of this. I should've told you."

"Pumpkin? What the fuck is a 'Pumpkin'? That's the second time I've heard that name. Henry called you that. I've been more than patient, but I demand some answers. How long have you been fucking Henry? This is some shit to get revenge on me. I knew it!"

"Tanner, this has nothing to do with revenge on you. And I'm definitely not fucking that . . . that man! How dare you! It's me . . . your wife! I've been raped . . . and . . . and all you can talk about is yourself?" I threw my arms up in frustration. "I should've confronted your issues when we first married. But I was just happy to have you paying attention to me. Now I guess it's too late. Your ego and indiscretions have been out of control. And don't think I'm still in the dark about you and Rory either."

"What . . . did you say?"

Pumpkin's bombshell was true. I knew as soon as his tone changed. "I know all about you and my *best friend*," I spat, the taste unappealing. "And your baby!"

Then he did something I'd never seen. He slapped me.

Already battered and besieged, I almost lost consciousness when I met the floor. I think the shock and stinging on my cheek kept me there. Tanner stood over me as I tried to right myself and crawl away. He peppered the top of my head with slaps, less forceful and more taunting this time.

"Did you do that to Rory? Did you throw that stuff in her face? Answer me, bitch, or so help me . . . !"

I balled up on the floor, cowering before his self-righteousness. I was his wife, yet he was defending the tramp who I thought was my friend. Pumpkin was right about me. I wished she were here now.

"No," he answered his own inquiry calmly. "You didn't. You don't have the balls to do that. Too soft, my little princess. Yeah. Way too soft. Probably would've dropped the bottle and run off. Did you pay someone? Uh-huh. Bet you did. With my

money too. Probably got that bum that you're fucking to do it."

The accusations were the final straw. I lowered
my hands from my face. Further assault be damned.
I was sick and tired of being sick and tired.

"I . . . I'm not sleeping with anyone, Tanner!
You're the only one who can't go a minute without
fucking or sucking something, you sick bastard."

He smirked.

"Not sleeping with anyone? Yeah. You're certainly not sleeping. Rape, my ass," he taunted.
"Ha! I can't believe I married a whore. I thought
I'd scouted way better than that. But you fooled
me, Bianca. Brava." Two claps over the ringing in
my head. Both of them false in their approval. "No
wonder you're always too tired to see about me or
my needs. You're too busy fucking the whole town
behind my back."

I was about to stand up when he hauled off and
punched me in the nose.

I slammed into the end table from the force,
enveloped mercifully by oblivion, where clarity
dwelled.

35

PUMPKIN

The door to my parents' bedroom opens all the way.

I hide behind Molly Wonder, holding her in front of me like a shield. If my dad sees her first, he might not be mad at me.

Molly Wonder protects me as my dad walks by. I knew she was magic.

He doesn't see us.

He looks drowsy, walks like the mummy from those scary movies.

I hate scary movies. They give me bad dreams if I watch them.

The cigarette he's smoking stinks. Like the time lightning hit the grass and it burned.

I would choke putting that near my mouth, but he doesn't.

I guess that's why my dad is super.

He goes in the bathroom to potty.

Mom must be awake.

Me and Molly Wonder run in the bedroom to say hi. She'll be so surprised.

I'm surprised instead.

The nice lady from the place with pancakes and pie is here. The one with the pretty yellow hair. She's walking around slowly like my dad, but she's smiling. Looks sleepy and happy.

What is she doing in their bedroom? Were they talking about me? Did I do something wrong and she came by to tell on me?

Does Mom know?

Yes.

She does.

She's in there too. Quiet and sitting on the edge of their bed. The sheets are all over the floor. I would get a spanking if my bed looked like that.

Why are they both naked? Are they about to take their baths?

And why is my mom crying?

"Bianca, what are you doing up?" my dad screams.

The noise frightens me. I drop Molly Wonder.

The commotion outside woke me up. I guess a sister can't get a rest these days. Tanner's voice can be so annoying. The punch he landed on my nose was worse.

Messing up my looks was a no-no. I heard him referring to Bianca as a ho. *Whore* was actually what he said.

The blood flowed from one nostril into my

mouth. I tasted some and smeared the rest, laughing at him all the while. Yep. Bianca was in over her head . . . again.

"Now you want to laugh? After all I've done for you?" he crowed. "A know-nothing, do-nothing from Seattle? You were slaving away in a fucking shoe store when I met you!"

"Taking over your grandparents' chicken business doesn't make you any better, you pompous goof. What did Rory call you? Oh, yeah. *Mr. Clucker*." I chuckled. "Did you know she used to call you that behind your back to Bianca? Or was that part of her 'act' for Bianca too? Cluck. Cluck."

"What's with the third-person references, Bianca? I didn't hit you that hard."

"I'm not Bianca, you dumb-ass." I rose, staring him down even though he was the larger figure. No matter. It was as if the longer I looked, the smaller he became.

For probably the first time, Tanner Coleman backed down, however briefly, from a confrontation. He raised his hands defensively, as if trying to cool off.

"Okay. Okay. Stop with the games. Now is not the time. You're scaring me."

"Is that what made you go off and hit my girl? Your precious Rory? Why it's always got to be the white girls?" I joked. In a baby voice, I continued,

"What was it, Tanner? She told you that you had the biggest dick she'd ever seen?"

I cackled while he snarled, reaching for me. I evaded him, not up for another punch in the face. As I dashed around him, careful not to turn my back, I offered some advice.

"I've been on a tear tonight. You may want to keep those hands to yourself, lover boy. Did she tell you? That she knows about you and Rory? And that bastard son you have with her?"

"Stop it! I mean it, Bianca! You're about to get seriously hurt, and it's not going to be my fault." He undid his necktie, wrenching it free until it dangled across his crisp white shirt.

"It's *all* your fault, even if you don't realize it. This is your world, Tanner. Remember? You should. You do everything to remind Bianca of it."

"So . . . let's see how this works. I'm supposed to be talking to someone other than my wife? You're supposed to be this 'Pumpkin' I've heard too much about today? I'll play along. Is that what you want me to call you? *Pumpkin*?"

"Yeah. Sure. Call me Pumpkin. Nice one, huh? Maybe one day I'll tell you how I came up with it. We'll have tea or something. Didn't really have a name . . . or the freedom to do what I do until last week. Thanks."

"Huh?"

"Don't worry your overworked peanut head. I'm just making up for lost time."

"By ruining my life? Is that what you're here to do?"

"Maybe." I smirked. "Or maybe I'm just here to look out for Bianca. There's so much shit she's incapable of handling."

"I see," he spat, hating my dual reference. We now played a game of ring-around-the-rosy with the furniture, neither one looking to gain a seat. When he moved, I countered, every action an opposite reaction on my part—survival for a moment longer. "So, you're the person I should be asking if my wife has been fucking around?"

"Yes . . . that you should be asking me. But I have a question first."

"What?" he snapped impatiently.

"Why fuck Bianca's best friend? I . . . we have our limits."

"Rory never was your best friend. I'm the one who had her go by your boutique that day!"

"Why?" The revelation surprised me. I couldn't hide it.

"Good business. Because if I'm going to be fucked over, I like to see it coming. You needed a friend, and Rory was my eyes and ears. That you were from the same city just fit even better. It all worked out."

"Until I found out."

"Yes. How did you?"

My turn to surprise him; I relished it. "The sex club."

"What?"

"Don't play dumb. Leaving your poor wife home that night while you ran out to indulge yourself with Rory. Yeah. I saw you."

"Wha . . . How?"

"Up close and personal. Lorenda's gone. I hear you need a new maid in your life. Maybe a masked French one would fit the bill."

"That was you."

"Mmm-hmm," I purred. "Shared the room, hell . . . the very bed with you. Oh. And so did Henry. That same poor fool you'd fired. Isn't the irony delicious? But to answer your earlier question—it was me who fucked him. Not Bianca. Fucked him well, don't you think? And now you're fucked. Guess Rory didn't help you see it coming after all. Cluck. Cluck."

"Oh, my God. You are insane." He fished his cell phone from his pocket and began dialing. He was so nervous, he dialed a wrong digit. I watched him clear it and start again.

"Go ahead. Make your call, Tanner. And before you cast judgment, who do you think you were with when you made Bianca play dress-up all those times and took her to the sex club? Who do you think has been giving it to you like that, daddy?

Surely not Bianca. You scare the hell out of her. And if I didn't like to fuck, you wouldn't have gotten half that much."

"You need help . . . whoever you are. I'm ashamed to have you as my wife."

"That's it. Kick Bianca to the curb. I warned her, but she wouldn't listen. Calls herself being in love. At least I kept her from being burdened with a baby by somebody like you."

"What are you saying?" He snapped the phone shut, ending his conversation.

I grinned, pointing between his legs. "Your low sperm count. Apparently that didn't stop Rory. Bitch must have been ovulating when you hammered her. Hmm. Or maybe he's not even yours. Definitely a pro."

"What did you do?"

"Shhh. Bianca might hear." I giggled. "Maybe I've had some freedom a little longer than she suspects. Amazing what you can find on the Internet to kill the fishies. Stuff that looks just like your daily vitamins."

"You . . ." He clenched his fists.

"You thought I'd let you get Bianca pregnant so you can leave her and her daughter again?"

"Again?"

"What?"

"You said 'again.' "

"No, I didn't."

"Yes. You did. And you said 'daughter.' "

"I . . . I. Oh."

I stumbled, on the receiving end of what Bianca went through when I asserted myself. I could hear her . . . feel her rage as our memories swirled and coalesced. Tanner took advantage, on me before I could regain control. Trapped in a bear hug, I felt the air being squeezed out of me. My ribs ached. Lungs burned. I gasped from the constriction. He tightened, like he intended to kill me.

I pleaded with Bianca to wait.

And bit Tanner's nose.

My teeth sank down to the cartilage and bone. He yelped, relinquishing his grip as crimson flowed onto the now-ruined shirt. When he turned his back to me, I dove forward. In the blink of an eye, I wrapped my hand around his tie, coiling it around his neck in a less than proper way. A designer noose, not by design. The two of us spun madly, a whirling dervish of hate locked to the death.

If he hadn't been so concerned about his nose, he could've flipped me off. By waiting, I'd cut off most of his air. I wrapped the tie tighter in my hand, held on . . . waiting. Praying was for those with hope. Bianca would've done that. I was born from a lack of hope.

His breathing labored, he ceased trying to unseat me. Instead, his fingers tried digging into the rare space between flesh and fabric, hoping to find some slack. None found, he dropped to one knee with me still aboard his back.

His wheezing evident, I pulled and twisted more. I'd gotten one foot into his back to give me leverage and now had his head bent back at an unnatural angle. He tried to reach for me, but was unable. I allowed myself a smile as I imagined a great beast felled.

The group of men in white outfits who poured into the apartment robbed me of my satisfaction. They looked like hospital orderlies, except larger and more stoic. I was quickly pried off Tanner, then sedated with a needle. Spent from the day's events, both I and Bianca gave in to its effects.

"Get her out of here! Now!" I heard Tanner gasp as fresh air returned to his lungs.

36

HENRY

"Somebody went off on his muthafuckin' ass. Kna'mean?"

"Yeah. I do," I answered the young onlooker. We gathered across the street, held at bay by police tape. The street itself was filled with a convergence of police cars, fire engines, and news vans whose telescopic antennas scraped the heavens. The burned, smoking remains of a house in this part of town was big news. This house, though, held particular significance.

Mr. Reyes was amenable once again, providing me his old four-door Mercury to make the trip. After Pumpkin's cryptic message, I had to see with my own eyes. The blocked streets, a ball of flame peering over their tree line, were a good indication that I was unprepared. Still I pressed on, intent on being a witness. Close up, the level of devastation was frightening, impressive even, considering the single person who had wrought it.

Next to the burned-out SUV, the coroner had retrieved a semicharred body from the wreckage. I strained to recognize the person it used to be.

"You with the news or sumthin'?" the lanky boy at my side asked. He had to be in his early teens. Probably knew everything that took place on this block.

"No," I replied, giving him as little as possible.

"Oh."

My attire, although casual for this evening, set me apart from the neighborhood. Mere nights ago I was afraid to be in Hunter's Green. A shame in that it was the place I'd grown up. Something I wasn't apt to share. Now, what I'd seen and experienced beyond its boundaries was enough to reshape my perspective.

As the lyrics go, "It's not where you're from, it's where you're at."

Amazing how a few days can change a person.

"You knew Kash?"

"Used to go to high school with him."

"Oh. You from around here?"

"Used to be," I answered. "Docket Street."

"Get out!"

"I'm serious."

"Damn. At least someone did good."

"Not necessarily," I answered, raising my cast in the air for him to see. "Do you know if he was in there?"

"Yeah. Money . . . I mean . . . my sister Monique told me."

The two of us exchanged a glance. The fire engine's flashing red lights reflected off our faces. "Is she okay?"

"Yeah. She tough. She'll be a'ight."

"Good."

"I'm glad the ghost lady got him."

I was perplexed until I remembered the fair complexion Pumpkin possessed.

The ghost lady.

She certainly was a phantom.

"Yeah. Me too," I finally replied.

Pushing their way through the lines, two of the recently unemployed—Kash's thugs—bumped into us. As I turned around, they glanced back, recognizing me.

I stopped breathing.

They gave a nod, signaling we had no further dealings, then pressed on.

I would've watched them longer, just in case, except a reporter was also milling about. I'd seen her before. Usually did big exposés on channel six. Coming upon us, she asked, "Do either of you know what happened? Maybe know a gentleman they call 'Kash'?"

"Naw," my friend answered.

"Never heard of him," I answered.

She lingered on me. I was a terrible liar. Sensing

that the bigger story was still out there, she smartly moved on.

I'd overstayed my welcome. My curiosity sated, I wished the boy well, then left before I became a caption.

There was one final trip before I returned Mr. Reyes's car.

The river churned below.

The guardrail restored, I stood with a foot atop it. On some weird urge, I returned to the spot where two lives diverged. I wondered what had happened before I'd followed her out here, but heeded her warning.

Things must've been strained between Coleman and her to have brought on the strangeness. But my addiction and irrational hatred toward her husband had sufficiently snuffed anything further between us.

A final fleeting look at the river that bisected this town and I returned to the car. I had a long road ahead of me.

I hoped Pumpkin would, if she were unable to forgive me, at least know happiness.

37

LAST WEEK

"**B**e here at nine."

"Okay. I will."

"And you know what I want you to wear?"

"Of course, Tanner. Have I ever let you down?"

"No, you haven't," Tanner obliged.

"And I won't tonight."

I was going to do him one better. I was going to arrive at his office early.

My bath out of the way, I quickly applied the vanilla-and-bergamot body butter I'd bought from Neiman Marcus. After rubbing it in from head to toe, I threw a dash of body glitter across my chest.

Getting all toned, glistening, and smelling good was only half my preparation.

The door across my bedroom was the other part. In the massive walk-in closet was where my secrets dwelled. All the tricks Tanner required to keep his interest up.

In the far corner, almost unnoticed amongst the rows of garments and shoes, was a special section.

I walked over to it, sifting through the assortment of clothes and costumes Mrs. Tanner Coleman wouldn't be caught dead in.

Normally.

I held the corset against my body, psyching myself up for what I had to do. As I squeezed into it, my breasts thrust upward as if erupting out the top. The black stilettos and garters added to the scandalous nature, but the finishing touches had yet to reveal themselves.

Tanner had a fondness for long hair, something he'd expressed to me shortly after we were married. I preferred my style and, not wanting the tediousness of a weave, found another option for these times.

In a tiny alcove rested a mannequin head, from which I carefully removed the affixed wig. Its long strands flowing over the bare skin of my shoulders, I was pleased with the fit. Mirror in hand, I adjusted it until only a trained expert could tell it wasn't a part of me. The small plastic case, almost unnoticed, was equally important. I opened it and removed the contact lenses one at a time. They were colored—a shade lighter than my normal brown.

Once they were inserted, I blinked, then took another look as my vision adjusted.

Perfect.

Almost like another person.

"Yes, indeed," I said playfully to the image I no longer recognized. I still didn't have a name for her. One day I'd have to come up with one. *Maybe something naughty*, I thought with a blush.

Grabbing my trench coat, I went out into the miserable weather.

Half-naked and simply wanting to please my husband.

At Tanner's building, the darkness was disconcerting. I should've called Tanner, let him know I was here, but I was a big girl. Taking the private elevator, I tried dispelling the troubling mood plaguing me. Something was familiar about it, though. It reminded me of the dreams I'd been experiencing. The ones I couldn't remember, but that left me ill at ease once I was jarred from my sleep.

The elevator opened. As soon as I disembarked, I was besieged by memories of my childhood.

My Molly Wonder doll was missing. My dad said I didn't need her. That was what he told me before putting me to bed. I didn't need Molly. Down the dimly lit hall, I walked toward the closed door. Their bedroom.

No. I walked toward Tanner's office. Past the empty receptionist desk and into the work area in back. Tanner was waiting for me. Just down the hall.

Or was it the hallway at my old house? And where was Molly Wonder? She was still missing. And I'd gone in search of her.

Dizzy, I paused to dispel whatever was happening. I was a grown woman now. Not a child. After a deep breath, I proceeded. When I reached his door, I undid the trench coat and flung it aside. Another night of sexual fulfillment for Tanner was at hand.

You are sexy, you are confident, you are hot, I reinforced as I turned the door handle.

I cracked it. And my world fractured.

Tanner . . . Tanner was busy. With someone.

Rory. My friend.

He was fucking Rory.

Seated proudly in his executive chair as she bounced on him. Her blond hair entangled in his hands. Her breasts bobbing wildly. His eyes closed. In the moment.

But it wasn't Rory I saw.

It was the waitress from the diner. The one with yellow hair.

And it wasn't Tanner.

It was my father. Dad.

And my mom.

She was there too. In the room. In the bed with them.

I saw her just as I did that night.

Weeping uncontrollably. In the bed with them. Watching them.

Just as I watched them.

In both cases, I ran before they saw me.

I was good at running. Then as now.

I fled Tanner's office, wanting to get as far away as possible. I had succeeded until I lost control on the winding road along the river.

I'd ignored the signs.

As I went over the side to a sure death, I banged my head on the steering wheel.

"Poor Bianca," I remember her saying as she came to rescue me.

38

BIANCA

"Oh, my God!" I screamed, waking up in a panic and unable to move anything other than my head.

I was restrained and in a strange place. A small room with white walls. On a hospital bed with straps constricting my wrists and ankles. Monitoring equipment was attached to me, just like at Saint Aloysius. Except I wasn't there.

"Help! Help me! Please!"

I was Pumpkin. I had done . . . things. I remembered. And it shook me to my core. Perhaps more frightening than my current predicament.

"Help! Help!" I yelled again at the top of my lungs.

Somebody finally answered. A middle-aged white woman peered through the door glass. Possibly a doctor, from her dress. A large male orderly unlocked my cage, granting her entry.

"Mrs. Coleman, how are you feeling?" She seemed

calm, even cheerful. A chart was in her hand, something written about me probably.

"Scared," I answered. "What am I doing here? Why am I tied up?"

"We're not here to hurt you. You're restrained for your own safety."

"I'm not a threat."

"That's not what your husband seems to think."

"Please. I don't want to be here. Where am I anyway?"

"We'll have plenty of time to talk about that. Right now we just need you to calm down. First off . . . are you Bianca Coleman?"

"Yes, of course."

"Good." She nodded, looking at the chart again. "I have someone concerned who wants to speak with you."

"Who? Tanner?" I asked. Despite my recollection, I wanted desperately to see him. Habit, I suppose. "Is he here?"

She didn't answer. Just pulled out a cell and dialed a number written on the paperwork she clutched. When someone answered, she held it to my ear.

"He's been worried," she assured me with a smile.

"Tanner!" I screamed as soon as he answered. "Get me out of here!"

"Calm down, Bianca. You're there for your own good."

"I don't want to be here. I don't even know where I am. Please. Come get me."

"I can't. Not yet, at least. I need to be focused for the mayor's appointment, so now wouldn't be a good time."

"Not a good time?" I echoed. "But . . . but I'm your wife."

"And you tried to kill me," he retorted. "But don't worry. I know you're not well and will be sure you are taken care of at the clinic."

"And then what? When can I see you?"

"Bianca . . ." He sighed. "I can't be a part of this madness. I'll be quietly filing for a divorce."

39

PUMPKIN

The doctor flinched when I awakened. I guess she was trained to notice those differences. Still the professional, she kept the phone to my ear. Either that or my being restrained gave her some balls.

I didn't care about her. I was too busy digesting what this motherfucker on the phone had just told Bianca.

"Divorcing her when things get hard. You're such a man, Tanner."

He laughed. "Playing that game again, Bianca? And you pretend to be someone else when things get rough. I think that makes us even."

"Why don't you bring your ass over here? I'll show you 'pretend.'"

"I refuse to be caught up in this insanity. Listen to the doctors and I'll be in touch."

"Tanner, you'll pay for this sooner than you know! Do you hear me?"

The doctor took away the phone, assured that any civil conversation had ceased. I listened to her quickly wrapping up with him, wondering what he was saying about me.

"Can you hear me, you bastard?" I yelled before she hung up. "You can't get rid of me! I'm going to get out of here!"

"Calm down, Mrs. Coleman. Please. I didn't mean for you to become agitated."

"Fuck you!" I spat at her, the wad landing on her lab coat. She retreated in the direction of the door. About to summon the apes, no doubt.

I tugged at the straps holding my arms at my sides. When they didn't give, I began shaking the bed violently. To and fro, it shook so hard that she became concerned. I felt a little slack around one of my wrists and began wriggling it free.

She saw the situation quickly changing and gave up trying to calm me down. She stuck her head out the door and yelled to somebody.

Two of the same monsters that had pulled me off Tanner rushed in as if just outside the door. The no-nonsense brutes pounced on both sides of the bed, quickly forcing me down on it. With her backup on hand, the doctor tightened the wrist strap, then administered a sedative into the IV at my side.

"No, no, no!" I screamed, feeling as helpless as Bianca for a change.

As I faded to black, I truly realized both of us were fucked.

Tanner may have won.

The only solace I had was that my final card hadn't yet been played.

That fleeting thought left me with a smile.

40

HENRY

I braved the cold this morning as well as the snow beginning to fall on Towne Square. Winter asserting itself. Its frosty bite being felt by all during this gathering at City Hall.

I flipped up my jacket's collar in response to the latest gust. The Starbucks across the street held a steaming chai tea reprieve just for me. I imagined its sweet, warm taste going down, but the reality would have to wait awhile longer.

This was what brought me out.

This was the show.

And I wouldn't miss it for anything.

I'd spent yesterday catching up on the world. I still needed a job, but with no one threatening life and limb, I felt at ease. Between the classifieds and searching Monster.com, I'd learned Tanner Coleman would be here.

Some kind of press conference about inner-city development. It appeared that in addition to being a dick, he also was Mayor Kurtz's "boy." That wasn't my concern.

I was here, blending in with the crowd, in hopes of seeing the man's wife. In spite of her warning.

Bianca Coleman.

I'd learned her true name.

Even spoken it aloud.

But in doing so, I didn't free myself of the demon's spell.

Yes, I'd done a lot of reading. Learned more about Tanner Coleman than I cared to know. Read up on the couple in the society pages. Saw the pictures of the two of them. So beautiful and adoring of each other.

All this made me wonder what pushed her over the edge; what would make a woman with seemingly everything go "Rice Krispies"?

Snap. Crackle. Pop.

My wit paused, Mayor Kurtz stepped to the podium before the assemblage—reporters, politicos, and representatives of the neighborhood Coleman was about to stick his foot in. The latter didn't seem overly thrilled. Perhaps things would quickly be warming up. Might be more fun than I expected.

I tuned out the standard introduction and formalities. Just focused on Coleman and wondered where she was. Maybe it was pointless to be here.

". . . the man who will head the revitalization of one of our failed promises. Because this entire city is marching forward together, not just the fortunate and affluent. And without further ado, I present you Mr. Tanner Coleman."

The applause was cordial. I decided to linger. Based on my studies, she usually was at his side at these sorts of things. Maybe he'd mention her in his speech.

"I just want to thank all of you for braving the weather today, as well as Mr. Mayor for appointing me to this very . . . very important task. For nothing is more important than taking care of our fellow citizens."

"What do you know about that, fat cat!" a heckler yelled. From the laughter, others agreed.

"You're entitled to feel that way now," he spoke humbly into the microphone. "But I just ask that you give me a chance. I came from humble beginnings too. Don't let my appearance fool you. Let my actions speak louder than mere words. Together . . . all of us can turn Hunter's Green around."

I bristled at the mention of the neighborhood. I didn't know how I'd missed that in the paper.

The response was half applause, half groans and mumbles. A lot of the concerned citizens weren't buying his act. Good for them.

Time for Starbucks for me.

I began moving toward the rear of the gathering.

A face I recognized raised her hand to pose a

question. The same reporter from channel six who had been nosing around outside Kash's that night. Damn, she got around.

"Yes, Suzette," he acknowledged, as if she were an old friend. Probably shared tea and crumpets with him and Bianca, no doubt. I kept moving, shuffling along.

"Mr. Coleman, where is your wife?"

I stopped.

"Excuse me?"

"Where is Mrs. Coleman today?"

"Odd question," he huffed. His reaction was even odder. I turned around to see if his facial expression matched his tone. "If you must know, *Suzette*, my wife is a little under the weather. She wanted to be here, but I insisted she get some rest. Now, do you have any questions about why we're gathered here today? I'll be more than happy to answer those as well."

The mayor chuckled at how smoothly Tanner had dispatched Suzette. Definitely the right man for this post, as far as he was concerned.

"Actually I do have some more questions, Mr. Coleman." She pulled out a notepad. One could tell she didn't need it. "Are you familiar with the area you're appointed to revitalize?"

"Yes. Of course."

"And its residents?"

"Well . . . some of them. But I can't be expected

to know everyone in Hunter's Green. I leave that to politicians such as the mayor."

He got a few laughs.

"And I understand that, Mr. Coleman. What I'm wondering about specifically is your connection to certain criminal figures in the area, particularly a man who was known as Kash?"

"I'm sorry." He turned his ear in her direction. "Who?"

"Um . . . a gentleman known as Kash . . . with a K. I believe you may have had some gambling debts with this person. At least until he and his associate were gruesomely murdered the other night and his house blown up."

"Suzette, I don't know where you get this kind of faulty information and wild conjecture, but I can assure you—"

"And is there any truth to the stories that your wife may have been assaulted by these figures before their murders and was recently hospitalized at Saint Aloysius as a result of such assault? Is that really why she's not here?"

Coleman stared her down, his hand suddenly covering the microphone. The mayor no longer looked so sure of his boy. In fact, he'd moved several seats down to ensure that he wouldn't be sharing any camera frames with Coleman.

The crowd began reacting to what was just thrown out by the reporter. A lot of them knew about Kash and his dealings. Now for Coleman and him to be connected, well . . .

It wasn't nice. Boos and impromptu chants began.

The rest of the mayor's appointees began fidgeting. Some looked absolutely nauseated.

As Coleman's hand reluctantly slid off the microphone, he addressed her.

"I said it before and I'll say it again. My wife is ill and that is all. And I don't appreciate these baseless accusations. I'm here for something positive and don't appreciate your cheapening it."

"We had ledgers delivered to our station, Newsmaker Six, anonymously. These ledgers, in fact, list you by name and some type of code, along with substantial sums owed over a five-year period. So you don't want to address—"

"Next question," he cut her off. "Maybe from a real journalist."

A hand came up as the mayor whispered to his handlers.

"Yes, Kip."

"Any truth to the allegations just raised, Mr. Coleman? And was Mayor Kurtz aware of your dealings before your appointment?"

They weren't going to let it go. A juicier story than what they came for. Even I could smell the blood seeping out of the steak.

I never knew he was on the line with Kash too.

Guess it wasn't my business to know. Still, I smiled with the newfound revelations.

Snowflakes clinging to my shoulders, I pulled my coat tight and left the circus for that overdue chai tea.

Man, I missed Pumpkin.

41

BIANCA

"In my dream, I'm back in Seattle. As a kid."

"Yes. Go on."

"I'm in the diner again. My dad comes here all the time. It's near Pike Place Market. I like the food."

She laughed.

"It smells good too. I guess that's why I don't complain much."

"Is anyone else there?"

"Bunches of people. It's the weekend. He made me miss my cartoons to come here. I think he brings me because my mom won't ask questions."

"Is your father eating?"

"No. He's here to see someone."

"Oh? Is it—"

"Yes. It's her."

"Is she nice to you?"

"Yes. Very. And I hate her for it. I hate myself too." I opened my eyes, uncomfortable with visualizing the moment anymore.

"Now?"

"Yes. Now."

"But how about then?"

"I thought she was sweet. Very pretty too. I remember the first time she spoke to me. She stopped talking to my dad and came over. She asked me if I wanted some dessert."

"Did you?"

"Of course. But my dad didn't like me eating too much dessert. He said it made me 'silly.' "

"Hyper?"

"He called it 'silly.' She ignored him, though. Asked me what I wanted. I wanted ice cream."

"How was it?"

"I didn't have it. Their freezer was broken that day. So she offered me pie instead."

"And?"

"I ate it. Loved it. Started asking for it every visit."

"You were there often?"

"Yes. Until she . . . began coming by our house. That was toward . . . the end. I really liked the pie. Can't stand the stuff now. I get sick at its smell."

"Apple? Cherry?"

"No. It was around Thanksgiving. Pumpkin pie. I liked it so much that she gave me a nickname. Started calling me—"

"Pumpkin," my therapist answered for me. For the first time in this session, we'd locked eyes. First time in any of these sessions.

"Yes. It's what she called me from that point on. Even when she took my dad away. He left me and my mom for her, y'know? After all the . . . things my mom did for him. Just trying to keep us together."

"Do you feel like you're to blame?"

"My mom wondered why the hell she'd call me Pumpkin. I explained that I'd been seeing her with my dad for quite some time. It just made my mom more depressed. Never treated me the same after that. She felt I'd betrayed her. All the way up until she . . . committed suicide."

"I'm sorry."

"Yeah," I said, grabbing a Kleenex. "I left Seattle a few years later. Just got on that bus one day . . . and came here."

"So . . . do you now understand how you may have developed this separate persona unbeknownst to you?"

"Yes. What did you call it?"

"Dissociative disorder. Although yours is quite complex, given the issues with your husband."

"Doctor, can you help me?"

"Yes. We can try, Bianca."

For the first time since being in here, I ceased looking at this person as my enemy.

I held out my hand.

And she took it.

Something to work on.

42

HENRY

I paced outside the treatment facility, an institute adorned with ivy snaking across its hallowed, aged exterior. Learning of her upcoming release, I acted irrationally once again. Couldn't help it.

It had been a long time, but that all too familiar rush greeted me. I plopped a piece of gum in my mouth to take the edge off. As I waited, I kept my distance beyond the walls.

Then the gate opened.

She wore a mahogany cardigan and a plaid skirt this crisp spring day. Classy and sexy she was as her brown suede boots strode down the worn steps toward the waiting limo. Rather than rushing to it and fleeing the place of her confinement, she did the unexpected—removed her sunglasses and paused to reflect. I think she was savoring the fresh air as much as I. As I crossed the street, the limo driver was putting the Lincoln in park. She motioned to him that she would be a minute. In the sycamore trees that lined the street, she watched the cardinals dart about overhead.

When she saw me, I froze. Yards and worlds apart, neither one of us knew what was going to happen.

"Why are you here?" she groaned.

She wasn't ready for this. Far too fragile for me to be intruding at this moment. Instinctually I reached out, but quickly withdrew my hand. It was free of pain, free of the cast.

"God, I really don't know. I . . . I just . . . My name is Henry," I futilely offered.

"I know. Now please leave me alone."

"Damn. My sponsor warned me against coming," I fretted, sharing my thoughts verbally.

"Sponsor?"

"Gambler's Anonymous. Y'know. My issue?" I shook my head. "Sorry. I keep thinking I'm talking to . . . You don't remember me, do you?"

"No, not really. Just that awful experience."

"This is bad. Really bad. I just don't know how to go forward without—"

"Let's cut to the chase. I'm not ready for this. You've been waiting for me to come out. Now what do you want from me? What more?"

"All I want is to thank you . . . or Pumpkin. You really did a lot for me, and I messed it all up. I just want to tell you that I'm working now and staying humble. I'm fighting my demons day to day, and

I've done well so far. I've been waiting for this day, when I could be face-to-face with you. I came to beg for your forgiveness, Pumpkin."

I bowed my head.

She just shook hers, the beginnings of a curse word forming, but she broke it off. The limo driver exited, watching both of us curiously. She nodded that she was ready, then turned to me.

"There is no Pumpkin, Henry. Move on. She was a creation . . . a fantasy. Neither she nor I are your salvation. I don't know you and don't care to know you. And I don't accept your apology."

"Oh. I guess I get what I deserve."

"You most certainly do. Actually, you're getting off light." A gleam formed in her eye. It was there for a nanosecond, then gone in just a blink. "Good-bye."

The driver came around, opening the door for her. As she entered, I felt a deep sense of loss welling up in me. Something dear was slipping through my grasp, destined never to be held again.

"Hey! Wait!" I called out before her door was shut. She just looked, her patience waning. "Pumpkin said she'd kill me if she ever saw me again."

The driver closed the door, leaving me staring at a tinted window. I smiled, searching for something on the other side. A sign of some sort. As the limo began pulling away, her window lowered.

My spirits lifted.

"Then consider yourself lucky that I'm not her," she replied as the limo pulled off.

Destination?

Unknown.

I just knew I wasn't going with her.

43

BIANCA

I did remember him.

Beyond the torture endured that night.

Bits and pieces. Like snapshots.

Sweet, stupid Henry. A foolish man fraught with wrong choices. With what I'd just done, I'd saved him one more.

"Ready, ma'am?"

"Yes. Get me away from here."

He scrutinized me in the rearview mirror, uncertain whether I'd changed my mind about the first destination on the itinerary.

"Go," I insisted. I folded my arms, averting my eyes before I said something rash. If only my life could be reconciled like my personality.

The limousine ride was quiet and reflective. I sifted through distasteful emotions against the backdrop of smooth jazz emanating from the speakers. Four anonymous instrumentals later, we were in the thick of it.

Hunter's Green. The wooden neighborhood sign was warped and faded, with only the word GREEN still prominent. A testament to failed policies and administrative apathy.

Tanner had been charged to fix this, but while I was . . . away, his glorious committee was scrapped. Tanner had gambling debts with the devil who had dwelled in these here parts. When the reports flew, he was cast off like Paris Hilton's last boyfriend. He was never charged with that evil man's murder, but implications sufficed. His empire was on shaky ground.

And shaky ground allowed for takeovers.

From what I read, his board of directors felt it was time to take the company in "another direction."

Suffocated aspirations.

Our journey took us past the charred shell of a home. Deep black marks were scoured into the driveway where vehicles once sat. Yellow streamers blew in the wind; tiny survivors of the police tape once strewn about. A warped shrine—not even the neighborhood felt it worth sifting through the rubble.

Not far from there lay a strip of town homes, just off the bus route on South Main. We stopped in front of the third one on the left, painted gray with a red-brick stoop. A man in a camouflage jacket sat next to the railing, sharing some time alone with his cigarette. We amused him. He took a drag . . . grinned, then repeated.

As I exited, he yelled to someone inside. Thin walls yielded the *thump-thump-thump* of descent from the second floor. Figuring it was who I came here for, I thanked him. Drag . . . grin, he went again.

"Sheeeed, rich folk crazy," he declared before extinguishing the Camel with his foot and departing down the block.

The front door swung open and the person I'd sought exited. She wore a plain white T-shirt and gray warm-ups that fit over her full legs. On her feet, she wore furry Elmo slippers.

"Maybe I should've called. I didn't mean to run him off."

"Oh. That's just my uncle. He acts like that whenever somebody stops in a limo. We get that at least twice a week around here."

Serious until her full lips broke into a smile, Deonté broke down. She sprang off the stoop, clearing the three steps easily to embrace me.

"I thought you weren't coming back. I'm so sorry about what happened with you and Mr. Coleman."

"I'm not." I chuckled. "It's okay. Really."

Breaking from our hug, I beheld my former assistant, embarrassing her when I lingered on the scarf that covered her hair.

"I really came to see how you were making out."

"You know me. I'm makin' it do what it

do. School's going well. Got another job since you . . ."

"Where?" I asked, feeling bad over the circumstances I'd forced her into.

'The SuperTarget across town."

"Oh."

"Yeah. I got on as a manager. I absorbed all that 'experience versus a purchase' mumbo jumbo you used to harp about. Making them all feel special out in the 'burbs."

We shared a laugh.

"I'm glad you landed on your feet."

"I did, but it's not as good as working for you."

"Really?"

"You took a chance on me, Mrs. Coleman. When you didn't have to. There were a lot of 'sure things' you could've chosen from my program instead."

"I knew who I wanted."

"Aww," she gushed.

"How are the grades?"

"A's. Just ready for graduation, y'know. Um . . . do you and your driver want to come inside? It's looking a little janky in there, but . . ."

I glanced at the driver. He was on his phone, probably complaining about where I had him at the moment. "I can't stay long, Deonté. I came by to offer you something."

"What?"

"Your own business."

"What?"

"All these 'whats,' " I teased. "Are you that rapper Lil Jon now?"

"What you know about Lil Jon? I . . . I . . . Wait, wait. Wait. What are you saying, Mrs. Coleman?"

"The boutique, complete with shoe inventory. I'm giving it to you. That is . . . if you want it. I mean . . . you seem pretty happy with Target."

"Do I want it? You're not shitting me, are you?"

"Not in the slightest."

"Then my answer is yes!"

Deonté screamed in my ear as she hugged me again. As the emotion subsided, I felt her grip relax. "But where are you going? What are you doing?"

"After the divorce, I need to get away from here. Clear my head. Of course, I would pop in to check on you and would be just a phone call away."

"I . . . I could never repay you," she said between the groans erupting from her throat. Both of us were becoming misty eyed.

"Repay me by making it a bigger success than I could. You've got it in you. I'm certain."

I told her my lawyer would be in touch, then gave her one last hug. Between the unspoken hints, she knew she might not see me again. I was never good at good-byes. Seeing I was finished—and that we were leaving HG—the driver was quick to exit his seat and open the door for me.

"To the airport, Mrs. Coleman?"

"Yes, but take your time."

Once I was away from Deonté and any other person somewhat familiar with me, a deep breath rushed through my lips. I turned the music up, then mixed myself a drink.

Mrs. Coleman.

A title for which I had no further use.

After his heart attack, Tanner was charitable enough to settle amicably without a messy, protracted divorce in the press. His public image tainted and his strength waning, he wanted nothing more than to get on with his imperfect family with Rory. Her eyesight had returned in one eye. Uncanny how she favored the woman who ruined my family all those years ago. No wonder my mind went screwy that night I saw her with Tanner. Something I'd repressed for so long.

I hear my dad's new woman passed away. An unfortunate accident back in Seattle. Something about a radio and a bathtub.

The day before I got on that bus and came here.

A shame.

A fucking shame, I thought, holding the sarcasm at bay. I tuned the music to something more uptempo.

A strip mall caught my eye as we drove by. A more urgent matter at hand than harping on the past.

"Turn around," I exhorted. After muttering

under his breath, he spun the elongated Lincoln around.

"Did I miss a turn or something?"

"Pull in here." I pointed. "I need to pick up something in there." The store carried everything from hair for weaves to beauty supplies . . . and wigs.

Leave it to this side of town to have a quality wig shop. I knew the right one was inside.

Waiting on me to claim it.

"I'll be right back."

"Mrs. Coleman, I can run you by a nice mall instead. Are you sure you want to go in there?"

"Totally. And stop calling me 'Mrs. Coleman.' "

"Sorry. What would you like me to call you?"

With a gleam apparent in my eye, I smiled.

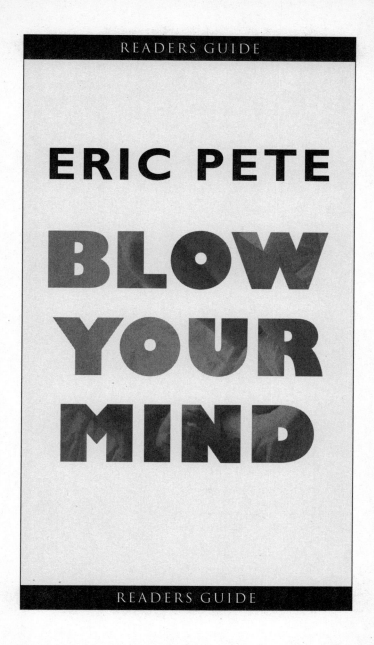

ERIC PETE

BLOW YOUR MIND

A CONVERSATION
WITH ERIC PETE

Q. Blow Your Mind is your sixth published novel!
Anything you want to say or get off your chest?

A. Wow. You're giving me a second to exhale,
huh? As I answer your questions, I'm remembering the day my very first novel, *Real for Me*, arrived from the printers. Six novels later, that joy
and anxiousness is unchanged.

Q. How did you come up with such a wild idea as
Blow Your Mind *in the first place?*

A. It's just some more of that random chaos that
took root. I'd kicked the scenario around for over
a year—of a woman role-playing for her husband
in an effort to please him, but who hits her head
on the steering wheel and gets stuck in the make-

believe persona—but wasn't sure I could carry it convincingly through a whole novel. Eventually, I decided, "What the hell!" I'll leave it to the readers out there to be the judges.

Q. *How long did it take you to write* Blow Your Mind?

A. Four to five months, which is funny, since I debated and debated over trying this story for longer than it took to write it. I guess it was the "right write." Feel free to slap me.

Q. *Which character was the easiest for you to write? Which was the hardest?*

A. I would have to say Pumpkin was the easiest, but also the most exciting. When you have a character you can just cut loose with, it's exhilarating. I just never knew what she was going to do next. For a change, the male character Henry was the hardest. It's usually the other way around. I wanted Henry to be loathsome in one breath, but someone you could empathize with in the next.

Q. *Give us some insight into the title. How did it come about?*

A. The working title was *Caution: Dangerous Curves Ahead*, playing off the car wreck at the beginning (and Pumpkin's literal *curves* . . . ahem), but it wasn't sexy enough. We wanted to play off the psychological elements and head games that take place in the story, but without giving away anything. *Blow Your Mind* fit like a glove. The title structure also was similar to my previous novel, *Gets No Love*. Afterward, I remembered stating in an earlier interview that I thought my upcoming project would blow the readers' minds, and here we are.

Q. *Take us inside the head of Eric Pete. What type of characters do you like? What influences the creation of those characters?*

A. Flawed. I thought you knew. Television shows like *Deadwood*, *The Sopranos*, *The Wire*, *The Shield*, and *Rome* are prime examples of where characters get to be of both virtue and vice. It's all about the layers and how you can show a character in both the harsh light of day as well as the shadows cast by a night-light.

Q. *What's next for you?*

A. More novels and a short story or two in upcoming anthologies. I still haven't given up on seeing these novels on the big screen, although some of the secrets in *Blow Your Mind* might be difficult to hide in a visual medium.

Q. Any remarks for your readers?

A. Yes. If you're truly enjoying these stories of mine, please tell as many people as possible to pick them up too. Word of mouth is still the most valuable tool to ensure your favorite authors continue to have their works available to you. And again . . . thank you for spending your time with me.

QUESTIONS
FOR DISCUSSION

1. Did you realize or suspect Pumpkin's secret? If so, when?

2. Were you surprised at when or how the revelation occurred?

3. How do you think things would've turned out if Henry hadn't rescued her in the beginning?

4. What do you think of the character Henry's development?

5. What do you think of Henry's relationship with Pumpkin? Do you think she had true feelings for him? Do you think his feelings for her were legitimate/genuine?

6. What do you think was Pumpkin's view of the world? How did it differ from Bianca's?

7. Other than appearance, what are some other differences you noticed between Bianca and Pumpkin?

8. Do you think there were instances of Pumpkin manifesting herself or controlling Bianca prior to the car wreck? Do you recall any that were referenced in the story?

9. What do you feel contributed more to Bianca's issues—her childhood past or her current relationship with Tanner?

10. Why do you think Tanner "selected" her to be his wife and not Rory?

11. Did you suspect Rory's involvement with Tanner? If so, why?

12. In what city did this story take place? Did you ever realize that it wasn't mentioned or named?

13. How did you react to Bianca's remarks about the fate of her father's girlfriend before she left Seattle?

14. Did the revelation at the very end surprise you?

15. What scene in the book was the most surprising to you? The most disturbing? Most humorous? Wildest?

16. Is there any one character from *Blow Your Mind* whom you would like to see more of in the future?

17. If you've read previous novels from Eric Pete, how do you feel this one compares? Is there any comparison?

18. *Blow Your Mind* has been described as a "dark, erotic thriller." Would you agree or would you describe it differently?

19. Do you feel the book cover was a good match, considering the nature of the story?

20. If *Blow Your Mind* were a movie, who would you like to see portray Bianca?

21. Have there ever been situations in your life where either you did or would like to have exhibited a different persona (i.e., "game face" in a difficult or uncomfortable situation)?

Don't miss *Essence* bestselling author
ERIC PETE'S
powerful novels

————————

LADY SINGS THE CRUELS

DON'T GET IT TWISTED

GETS NO LOVE

————————

Read on for special sneak peeks
at Eric's sexy and gritty tales. . . .

Lady Sings the Cruels

"**Y**our girl gonna win, Bodie?" Ro asked in his laid-back drawl, thick like molasses from a can.

"You know what time it is. Think somebody out here got a better voice?" I answered over the screwed and chopped verses of Prince's "The Beautiful Ones." The trunk of the old Cadillac convertible rattled violently with each lazy note as if about to fly off its hinges. My niggas, the Fontenot brothers, rode up front, tossed back on that syrup. When they were mixing the codeine 'n' shit, I passed. *Need my head on straight for my boo, Amelia*, I proudly thought. She was downtown at the Four Seasons tryin' to change things in her life, so why shouldn't I?

"That show's full o' shit, if you ask me," Aaron volunteered as he wheeled the big orange slab down North Main, his normally blue eyes dyed bloodshot red from all the drank he'd been hittin'. Both the Fontenot brothers looked like white boys if a nigga didn't know better. I guess that's why they were always overcompensatin' 'n' shit—permanent scowls and always ready to break a nigga down if they got outta hand.

"That's just it. Nobody asked you," I snapped back. Ro laughed but you could barely hear him. He'd plopped a couple Xanax in his drank back at the crib. Even with all that, only half his edge had been taken off. Of the two, he was the scary one. If Aaron was the sound, Ro was most definitely the fury.

Aaron continued in spite of me. "Them stupid TV shows all outta a nigga's control 'n' shit. Dressin' folk up like some dolls and makin' 'em sang that gay shit. Who wanna hear some Barry fuckin' Manilow? Ya know? Shit ain't real like it is out here. What we do is real. If one of them judges came up in my face, tellin' me how bad I handle my business, I'd show him he's a wrong motherfucker. One time." He looked around for his Glock .40 to wave for emphasis, but couldn't find it. I just shook my head.

"Just drive, man. I wanna pick this up before she finishes. I wanna see her face when she walks out from her audition and I plant that boulder on her finger. Ya know?"

At the EZ Pawn, Aaron and Ro let me out the car so I could handle my business. Abdel, the Arab cat I'd been dealing with, recognized me and buzzed me in when I rapped on the door. I'd been to his store three times this month, putting some ends down on my shit. Well . . . Amelia's shit.

I was a Northside nigga and Amelia was a Southside girl from Missouri City, or Mo City as we called it here in Houston. She was my ride-or-die chick and had put up with much noise from me since we'd met. We'd almost broke up again last week when I realized she was out for good if I didn't quit my ways. Sometimes a nigga gotta burn shit out his system, y'know? I ain't gonna front. What I was gonna do today was big. Life changin', y'know? Yeah, I was scared.

I was giving Abdel a pound when Ro and Aaron caught the closing door. He stared at them, thinking they were white boys at first . . . and in the wrong neighborhood, until I spoke.

"They with me, bruh," I vouched, exchanging a look that told him not to sound an alarm or reach for whatever he kept behind the glass case. They were supposed to stay in the car, but true to their nature they did whatever the fuck they wanted.

"Oh," he replied. As he watched their demeanor, he smiled, realizing he'd been fooled by their features.

"Yeah, they's niggas too. Got that Louisiana shit in 'em." I laughed, just low enough for them not to hear. They were prowling around the other cases, eyeing all the good shit people had pawned. Abdel had clued me in on my last visit. High-end niggas losing their jobs at Enron had allowed gutter niggas like us to get high quality for cheap.

I reached in my pocket, pulling out the fat roll of

bills to seal the deal. Abdel's eyes lit up at the sight. He still had some reservations about my boys fawning over the items behind the glass, but went in back to get the ring for me.

"Damn, look at that one," Aaron said to Ro, bringing his attention to a bunch of new jewelry on display. The glow reflected in his hazed eyes.

Ro shuffled over in his white tee and baggy jeans and scratched the brownish-blond fuzz on his chin. He nodded as if responding to voices unheard by the rest of us. His gaze was clear and focused when he twisted slowly in my direction. "Bodie, why you didn't tell us 'bout this here?" he asked.

" 'Cause I know how you crazy motherfuckers be actin'," I replied. In fact, the only reason I was catching a ride with them today was because 1) they were my boys and 2) my Lac was off Westheimer getting dipped in some fresh candy paint. A lapse in judgment was nothin' new on my part. I'd have Amelia's ring soon, so it didn't matter.

"How much you payin' for her shit?" Ro asked. I held up the fingers, each one indicating a grand.

"Daaamn," Aaron gushed. Ro said nothing.

Abdel came back with my ring in a jewelry box. "She's going to love this," he said. He opened it, allowing me to inspect. I didn't trust anyone when it came to matters of money. I held the solitaire up to the light and my world changed.

As slow as the Fontenot brothers had been previously, it was like someone lit a fire under them. I'd seen that fire in action before. And it was nothin' nice. Abdel's eyes spoke to me as I paused from admiring the ring I was to propose with. His gaze met mine, wondering how I could betray him. I was shaking my head in denial when Ro's 9 mil swung across his head, leveling him. Dumbstruck, I just stood there.

"Don't even think about an alarm, boy." Ro slid around me like I was a store fixture and hopped the counter in one smooth move. He leveled his 9 on Abdel, on whom he'd opened a nice cut. Aaron followed his brother's lead. After checking the front door, he pulled out his gun. I guess he'd found his Glock after all. They were wildin'.

"You gettin' that ring for free, bruh," Aaron gleefully proclaimed. "And then some."

Abdel began pleading for his life, to which Ro shouted, "Shut the fuck up!"

"Get the tape, bruh! Get that shit!" Aaron yelled at me. I didn't come here for this, but the time for talk was done. Without hesitating, I was back in that fucked-up mode too. Abdel wouldn't be telling anyone anyway. Not if he didn't want us coming back to pay him a visit. I stowed Amelia's ring in my pocket and ran to the video recorder in the back office. Coming from the front of the pawnshop, I could hear cases being shattered and glass shards tumbling to the floor. The store tape was in my hand when I looked at my watch. I was gonna have Aaron drop me off at the Four Seasons when we got outta here. It was a "when." An "if" never crossed my mind. It should've.

"Check for the money while you're back there!" one of them urged as I left the office. My stupid ass listened, stopping to look around. On Abdel's junky desk, I saw a framed photo of his family. I didn't get a chance to find anything else.

A raucous scream I recognized as Ro's rang out. I heard Aaron curse before the alarm went off and shots rang out. I dropped the tape and ran back to investigate. On the floor behind the counter lay Abdel's twitching body, a piece of his head having been blown off. In his dying grip, he held one of those taser guns. Aaron was helping a limping Ro out the front door and didn't even bother looking back for me. Torn between wanting to help the dying man and get the fuck away, I went on instinct and ran like O.J. It would've been all good except my foot caught the blood gushing from his wound. Slipping, I took an express trip to the concrete floor, where my head hit with a hollow thud.

It took a second for me to get back up and shake it off, but by then I could hear the loud exhaust on the orange Lac as it sped out the parking lot. Fuck this. I wasn't getting tagged for something that wasn't my idea. Alarm still blaring, I burst out the front door and ran for daylight.

Just make it home, was what my racing mind repeated again and again.

"On five!" he hollered.

The corrections officer, or CO, at the end of the row repeated him. The second time in two weeks my cell had been through shakedown. I came closer to check things out.

"Don't know why you're diggin' around my mattress," I said, looking over his shoulder. I maintained a safe distance while, on his knees, he checked the mattress frame for a shank. "You won't find nothin'."

He didn't answer but, finishing his inspection, moved to my pictures pinned on the cell wall. Winters, a CO about the same age as me, was better than most motherfuckers. Some of them liked makin' your life a living hell. He made sure you knew he was just doing his job. That earned him a nigga's respect on most days.

Winters lifted the pictures, making sure no contraband was hidden behind them. We weren't supposed to put shit on our walls. He could've been a dick and yanked them down. When he lowered them back in place, he stared at my girl's for a sec. Next to a wrinkled picture of my custom Lac was a picture of Amelia taken a year before I went away. She was just a young'un then, posin' all seductive in this camisole I'd gotten her.

"Nice, bruh."

"Ain't she though."

"Waiting for you when you get out?"

I laughed. Ten years is a long time. "I dunno. Ain't seen her in a minute. She special though."

"Sure seems like it," he muttered before moving on.

Winters thumbed through the pages of my book, *The Autobiography of Malcolm X*, leaving the page I'd marked undisturbed. Rather than tossing it on the floor, he handed it to me. "Great book," he said. "Sure made me get my act together. Maybe if you'd read it sooner, you wouldn't be in here."

I wanted to punch him for trying to talk down to me, but it wouldn't have done any good in the long run. Each day on the inside was helping me understand how I should handle things on the outside.

After sentencing, I'd done my first two years in Huntsville before being transferred to this new facility by the airport. Every day, I'd hear the planes flying overhead, imagining I was on one of them in a first-class seat to Mexico or maybe Rio for Carnival, where bronze, boomin' asses would shake in my face all night long. Yeah. Prisons are a booming crop in Texas, and folks like me are the seeds they water to make them grow.

"Close five!" Winters hollered, his search completed. My cell door clanked shut. Before he left, he lingered by the bars. "Don't mean to preach, Bodie."

"S'all right. I know. Instead of 'hangin' with you, I should be with my girl on the outside. She could sing her ass off, y'know? Without even tryin'."

His face grimaced. "She doesn't sing anymore?"

I paused. "No."

He didn't say anything else. Just moved on to the next cell on his list.

I set the book down to fix my mattress. As I bent over, I heard a tapping sound behind me. I thought Winters had returned and expected to hear his voice.

"Nice ass, Antoine."

No one but my grams called me by my birth name. And this bitch wasn't my grandmomma. I ignored her and kept putting things back in place.

"Ain't gonna talk to me, Antoine?" I heard her say something into the radio on her shoulder. My cell door started opening. I counted to ten before acknowledging her.

"Cell check," CO Arnold proclaimed as she stood there, ready to mace me if I got out of hand. The HNIC on this block, she was one of the worst ones. Don't get me wrong. Arnold was fine as fuck. She was around five-six, the color of a good cigar, and thick in the hips, and her hair was always done up. Today, she rocked one of them bought ponytails. I would've tapped that country ass on the outside. But because she was an evil ho who liked making life miserable for niggas on the inside, she was never getting it from me. That seemed to make her angrier.

"Winters just came through," I snapped, knowing she really didn't care.

"And it looks like he missed something."

I looked around the tiny space, imagining some crevice he hadn't touched.

"There," she said, pointing at the wall near the head of my bunk. My pictures.

She kept her hand on her radio, daring me to make a sudden move to stop her. I wasn't getting my head caved in today. She smiled as her leg brushed against mine. I wanted to trip her.

"You know you're not supposed to hang anything on the wall."

I raised an eyebrow, keeping my hands on the bunk and my mouth shut.

She snatched down the pictures of my Cadillac and Amelia and looked on the back of each.

"This your car?"

"Yeah."

"This your girl?"

I nodded my head, not really knowing anymore if Amelia was "my girl." Her last visit had ended with us screaming at each other across the table.

"Which one of your boys you think is fucking her now?" I bit my lip. She saw my eye twitch and laughed. "*Manslaughter?* You're gonna be here awhile, Antoine. You might as well get used to things."

The picture of my Lac, she balled up and dropped on the floor. Amelia's picture, she slowly ripped in half before letting the pieces fall as well.

"Oops," she said with a shrug. "You better pick that trash up. You know we don't allow littering."

I was putting the pieces of Amelia together when I heard, "Close five!"

"97.9 The Box. Can't stop, won't stop. You're on the air."

"Yeah. I wanna hear that new song from Natalia."

"Well, we're giving it to ya! That new joint from Houston's ooooooooown Natalia!"

I was trying to get to my waitress job at Mirage, but when I heard it, I focused on nothing else. The cars honking on the 610 Loop went silent. The construction crews hammering away on the latest expansion project disappeared. All that was there was me and the voice, the voice of my best friend.

"Yeah!" she screamed frantically as she emerged from the ballroom that day. It was as if the Holy Ghost had jumped inside her and wouldn't let up. She was crying uncontrollably and the cameras were eating it up. I was so happy for her; I ignored the number pinned to the front of my blouse and began jumping too.

"You did it! You did it!" I screamed as I ran, embracing Natalia hard enough to crush her.

"I'm going to Hollywood, Amelia! I'm going to Hollywood!" She then went into another fit, which made the other *U.S. Icon* contestants either nervous or happy, depending on their mental state. It didn't matter to her because she'd made it past the preliminaries. Hollywood and all that TV exposure awaited. It didn't matter to me because she was my best friend . . . and my time to shine was coming up. At her mom's house the night before, we'd discussed how we would handle it when we were the final two contestants on *U.S. Icon*. We were going to handle it with dignity and class. No catfighting or backstabbing. Yep. Represent for H-town. Beyoncé had already gotten hers. Both me and Natalia remembered running into her and the rest of them girls at talent shows around town. She had the looks and her momma 'n' 'em behind her, but we had the voices. We were on the come-up now.

Natalia wiped her eyes as she came down to Earth. She'd quit hyperventilating. A lady behind us who'd been rejected was pitching a fit and now stealing the show. The cameras rushed with great zeal to cover every single curse word. Natalia rolled her eyes. "Girl," she said as she tried to put her matted hair in place, "they're going to be calling you in there soon."

"How were they? How did they act? What did they say?"

She laughed at my bombardment. "Well, that

one guy, the asshole from Europe. He kept a straight face the whole time. I know I blew him away, but he tried to play it off."

"Wow."

"Yeah, girl. We're going to Hollywood!"

I felt uneasy when she included me. I hadn't gone before them yet. They might have reached their quota of fine young sistahs from the South. Well, they were just gonna have to make room for one more.

One of the production people called out my number to let me know I'd be going before the judges soon. Natalia had been holding her pee all morning and ran off before she burst. I felt a case of nerves coming on and tried to breathe.

Bodie promised he'd be there, but he wasn't. Just like him. *Either high or sleeping off a high,* I thought. He'd let me down so much, but I was stupid enough to get involved with him. One of them Northside knuckleheads he was—dangerous and with plenty of money I never asked about. He treated me like a princess whenever he was trying to make up. I was finished with making up. He wasn't here when I needed him most. It was time to move on.

The contestant just ahead of me was called into the ballroom. I watched her give her parents a final hug. On the wall above her, the Four Seasons hotel had a TV monitor affixed to keep us hostages entertained and off the show's back. I noticed KPRC interrupting for late-breaking news.

The scene switched from *The Golden Girls* to a shot from their news helicopter as police cars chased a black man on foot. Other than a white T-shirt, I couldn't make out a thing about him other than his quickness. He did *something* stupid, I thought. It would've been easier on him if he just quit running. The scene was a replay from earlier and was just being reaired. Losing interest, I looked around for Natalia again. She was still in the bathroom or maybe on the phone with her boyfriend.

When I looked back, the details were scrolling across the bottom of the screen. Someone had tried to rob a pawnshop. Somebody had been shot. The production assistant signaled me that it was time to go to staging. I lingered a second longer to see the suspect. His arrest photo flashed, filling the entire screen. *Antoine "Bodie" Campbell* was the name displayed beside his image.

"*Ma'am*, you're up next," the production assistant repeated with emphasis.

Natalia's new song ended, bringing me back in the now. She'd called me from Miami last week wondering what I thought of her new CD. I lied to her and said I thought it was the bomb. I hadn't bought it. I was gonna have to get it soon, but couldn't bring myself to just yet. Besides, I was late for work . . . again. I sped up, but knew I could never outrun the thoughts running through my head.

Don't Get It Twisted

"911. How may I help you?"

"I need the police!"

"What's the nature of your call, ma'am?"

"Can you please just send the police! And an ambulance too!"

"Ma'am, please stay calm. I just need to get some information from you. Is someone hurt?"

"Yeah, you could say that. A couple of people."

"What happened?"

"What happened? Lady, will you fuckin' hurry up! People are hurt and bleeding!"

"I'm dispatching them to your location in Long Beach as we speak. I need for you to remain calm, okay?"

"Okay! Okay! I'll try."

"Now, I need to ask you a few questions. Do you know who is responsible for this?"

"Yeah. Me."

"Ma'am? Ma'am, are you still there?"

"Yeah. I'm here."

"I need your name."

"Isrie. Isrie Walker."

.   .   .

"Hello?" I said into the receiver. Nothing. The caller ID showed a blocked number. Should've known it was nothing but trouble.

I called out again and was met with still more silence. As I went to hang up, I heard laughter—a woman's laughter. I would've hung up—no, *should've* hung up—but now I was curious. "I can hear you on the phone, so you might as well say what you have to say."

There was a click as she put her phone on speaker. Blocking out everything, I could now hear a man's steady breathing. There was a rustling sound as if sheets were sliding around. The woman groaned, not from pain, but from pleasure. He was fucking her. Ryan was fucking her and they had the nerve to call me to hear.

I can't believe this shit, I thought to myself.

"Oh, yes! Get that shit. Get that shit, daddy," she urged him. Damn. I knew he would get it too. That was never my problem with him.

Ryan and I had been seeing each other for the past five months. *Had* is the operative word. I'd dumped him last night. Tonight, we were supposed to see that Denzel Washington movie. Instead he was fucking the girl who thought she'd won the ultimate prize and I was on the phone like a fool.

"Ooh!" she gasped, startling me out of my funk. "No, no. Don't do it like that. Ryan, you're gonna make me scream."

I knew what *that* was and had had enough. "You're welcome to my seconds, bitch!" I was about to click my phone off, but raised it back to my mouth. "And for the record, I dumped him!"

Rebelling against my parents' nagging to find a man and settle down, I'd met Ryan. He was my date on one of those television dating shows where they pay you to go out with a complete stranger. Turned out Ryan was no ordinary date, but a flashy record producer out for some publicity.

I was extremely skeptical when I met him, but those dreamy green eyes and peanut-butter-smooth skin had me ignoring the obvious. Ryan was a bad boy. The good that came with that in the bedroom . . . and on balconies . . . and in a restaurant bathroom once also came along with the paternity tests and threats from crazies like the one on the phone. Ryan had too much ego. It was that ego that caused me to let him go last night after complaining I was fed up with the loose ends, or as I preferred to call them, tired-ass hoes. His ego lost, but why was I the one feeling so ripped up over it? I was never one to depend on a man to define who I was, so I decided to brush my shoulders off like the pimp that I was.

I dumped the pint of Ben & Jerry's in the sink

and went to change. Some Italian mules, a pair of my favorite denim jeans, topped off with a black long-sleeved tee, and all that was left was my grille. I went into my bathroom, turned on my makeup light, and went to work.

When finished, I was dressed and made up with nowhere to go. I still could have gone to the movies without Ryan, but decided to have a drink at a local spot. I wasn't one for drinking alone, so the call went out.

I speed-dialed a number, then waited. My girl, Deja, was always working late on her photo assignments, and it was easier to page her and let her get back to me. Five minutes later, my phone rang on cue.

"Hello?"

"What's wrong, Isrie?"

"You know me too well, D-Square." Ms. Deja Douglas got her nickname from both her initials and her cup size, although she was actually a large C or small D.

"I thought y'all were going to the picture show tonight." *Picture show.* Deja always had to be different.

"No. I'm about to go have a drink, though. Want to come?"

"On a Monday?"

"Look, I'm dressed up and don't feel like staying in the house. Are you coming or what?"

"All right. I'll keep you company, but I'm not drinking anything heavier than water with lemon. I have a shoot in the morning. Look, I've got one more roll to develop. How about in thirty minutes?"

Gets No Love

The smell of gunpowder burned my nostrils while I tried to stop the bleeding. "Shhhh. Don't worry. I got you," I whispered as tears streamed down my face. I didn't know if my words were being heard, but it didn't matter. Saying them was all I could do to make myself feel sane at the moment. The sirens were getting closer, but the screams from everyone in the park drowned them out as the reality of what had just occurred set in. Some people wouldn't be going home from today's picnic. A Saturday, of all days.

"Nooooooo! Please, Lord! No! Not another one!" It was Mrs. Dumas's familiar, crackly voice screaming frantically. I pulled myself out from my haze to watch her slowly inch herself out from under the large limp body that draped her.

"Lance?" The woman I held gasped. Her voice was faint.

"Yeah. I'm here."

"Am I going to die?"

"No," I replied, looking down into her vacant

eyes and at my shaking bloodstained hands. "I won't let it happen."

"Y-you can't always save everyone, Lance."

"I know," I said, glancing around at my many failures. One, in particular, would go down as my greatest failure. His eyes, finally at peace, were still open and boring into my soul as Mrs. Dumas cradled him to her bosom.

Rest in peace, dear friend, I mouthed silently.